Between the Lines

Sarah Foster

First printing
ISBN: 1-4137-6022-8
PUBLISHED BY PUBLISHAMERICA, LLLP

Second Printing   2022
ISBN: 978-1-946205-99-5
Published by Ladies of the Lakes Publishing

Printed in the United States of America

Dedicated to the people who make it
possible
for me to keep on writing:

Brian and Tyler Timm
Betsy Gibbs
Heather-Lee Lafferty
Jonnie Schwersenska
Morris Striplin, for your contributions to this
book.

2022
Tony Foster, for all of it. The mighty cables,
Scotland. Eleven!
No Limits.

4

Acknowledgment

I would like to thank Morris Striplin for writing the rather "risqué" parts of the book. He did an excellent job fitting them right into the story. He did an excellent job helping me through my divorce and helping me keep my head up and keep on writing and not let anyone or anything get me down. Thanks, Strip. You are a true friend.

ONE

Thank goodness the ceiling fan was working and there was a nice breeze off the Gulf. Otherwise, I would have sweated my ass off because another blackout had burned out the fuses and I was in no mood to get up and go buy more. I was lying back in my lounge chair trying to drift off to sleep while Sarah went for a dip.

For some unexplained reason, I couldn't get the triple-X film we had enjoyed together the night before out of my mind. We had done everything in the film more than once. I got off twice while I lost count for her, but what she whispered in my ear before she fell asleep was graphic enough to let me know she was more than satisfied with my performance. As the scenes ran across the screen of my mind, sleep was something I could not accomplish. In addition, my manhood was rising up, demanding my immediate attention.

It wasn't long before I knew he wasn't going to let me alone until we had traveled down that road again. Even my balls were beginning to anticipate the action. Without thinking, I found my hand inside my shorts squeezing and stoking my enormous hard on.

Just when I was going to pull my shorts down and go for broke, she backed into the cottage, pulling the sliding door closed behind her. When she turned, in that split second, Sarah must have guessed what I was about to do, for she smiled, reached around back untied and dropped the top of her bikini to the floor. Once we were staring at each other with lust in our eyes, she put her thumbs inside the front of her bikini bottoms and began to seesaw the front up and down, playing peek-a-boo with the top of her pubic hair.

She smiled when she saw the strained look on my face. Sarah knew full well my fondness for her thick, blonde pussy hair. In deference to me, she didn't even do a bikini cut. She just let it all hang out just for me.

Once she had pulled the bottom down far enough to expose her beautiful pussy, I could take no more. Raising my hips, I pulled my shorts off and tossed them on the floor and held my arms out to her. Sarah came running over, her generous brown breasts with hard, pointed nipples, bouncing as she giggled with anticipation.

When Sarah went down on her knees and reached for my throbbing erection, I caught her hands. That would have to wait until later. I would have dropped the ball the second I felt her tongue, and this time at least, I wanted to feel her warm wetness accompanied by the soft tickling of her pussy hair on my balls.

Sarah must have read my thoughts because she got up and straddled me. Reaching down, she gently took my rock hard erection and slowly inserted him. The sensation caused each of us to catch our breath before we could go on. After making sure I was completely lubricated, we started a gentle rhythm, building and ending in a mutual, screaming orgasm.

Alex slammed the book shut and downed the glass of ice water sitting on the coffee table in front of her before she slouched back in her chair and let her fingers find their way down her thigh, into her hot succulence below. All she had on was her silk robe and nothing underneath, her favorite attire while she was reading a Sterling Morris novel. His latest, *Summer Rain* had her quivering every time she picked it up. She let her fingers dance until they found what they were looking for. She leaned back and let out a whimper, which soon became a moan as her fingers took control and just went faster and faster until she was able to satisfy herself. Her scarlet red lips parted as she let out one last cry, her icy blue eyes closed. When she was through, she brushed aside her long raven black hair, picked up her book with a devilish smile and walked into her kitchen.

Alexandra Tate was the owner and rumored ice queen of Tate Publishing. In reality she *was* a ruthless businesswoman, but only to protect her fathers great name. Alex grew up in the small town of Highland, IL. Her mother had passed away during childbirth, so Edward Tate was the only person she was ever able to love. He was lonely without his wife there but did all he could to keep his daughter happy. They were poor, as he was a starving author. He wrote and wrote and wrote. The house was filled with manuscripts, but none of them were ever published. Most of them were never even submitted. He passed away when Alex was only nineteen, leaving her with his collections. With nothing but a computer, a desk and a website, Alex started Tate Publishing. She had enough work of her fathers to keep her busy for months, until she got clientele built up. Her father's books soon reached the top sellers list and skyrocketed. Ten years later, Tate Publishing was one of the largest publishing houses in the country, located in the heart of Jackson, Tennessee.

Jackson held no special meaning back then to Alex, she loved the South and wanted to experience it herself. She got out a map one day and decided that was where she was going to live. With Tate Publishing as her fortune, she had a replica built of the Jefferson Plantation down in Alabama. She really loved the South and tried to live it as much as possible. The men down here were sweet as sugar to her. They were nothing like the men in Illinois. These men were true southern gents. They were polite. Not just use your manners polite, they knew true southern hospitality. She loved this town and never planned on leaving. She got accustomed to their sweet tea and their slower paced lifestyle. She was used to everyone being in a hurry all the time. She had learned to relax a little and take life easy once in a while. Until it came down to business of course. No one dared step foot in her way in her company. She had watched it grow from scratch and there was nothing that was going to get in her way to run it down.

TWO

Sterling Morris took another drag off his pipe and sat back in his leather recliner. He glanced around his office. This was the life. As soon as his next book hit the bestseller list he was sure to strike it rich. He was not just interested in money; he just wanted to be well known for his writing. He was known all right, but not known enough. He had some psycho fans out there who sent him pornography and shit like that but that is not the kind of person he was. If he wrote himself into his books, they would all be sappy romances and he just could not do that. He loved writing things that made people wriggle in their seats. He was just about to throw out another chapter or two when there was a loud knock on the door and then it flew open before he could get a chance to answer. It was Jackson Ripley, his editor and best friend. He was upset or excited about something, walking around the office like someone had just taken his prized possessions.

"Do have a seat, Jack, by all means, come right on in." Sterling sat back in his chair again waiting for his friend to calm down.

"Sterling, we have a problem." Jack finally sat down and put his elbows on his knees and his hands on his face. He truly looked flustered.

"What the hell has gotten into you Jack? Jesus Christ, calm the hell down. What's going on?"

"As of fifteen minutes ago, Advent Publishing belongs to Discovery Printing." Jack stared at Sterling for a reaction but there was not one.

"What are you talking about, Jack? Cliff would never sell the damn company!"

Sterling threw his pen on the desk and cringed at Jack. He knew, just by the look on his friends' face, there was bad news coming.

"He would if his little boy was just diagnosed with Leukemia and he sold everything to spend the rest of his life with his kid." Jack just sat there staring at Sterling, who had gone pale. His friend and publisher had a nine-year-old little boy, like a nephew to Sterling, named Justin. Justin was the greatest kid he ever knew. And now he has Leukemia.

"Holy shit, Jack. When did he find out? Why the hell didn't he call me?!" Sterling did not even wait for an answer from

Jackson Ripley; he grabbed his coat and ran out of his office heading towards his Monte Carlo. Once inside, he screeched the tires all the way down the street headed for downtown Milwaukee. Jack just sat there, staring after his friend, knowing he was going to see Clifford Ardent.

Half an hour later, Sterling was at Cliff's office sitting in front of a man who had just found out his son had this awful disease. He did not know what to say. Cliff looked awful. Sterling could tell he did not sleep the night before.

"Cliff. Why the hell didn't you call me, man?" Sterling wanted to be there for his friend.

"Sorry Sterling. All I could think about was *what if I was at work when my boy dies, or for his chemo?* I need to be there for him Sterling; he needs his mother and me. I can't stay with the company. I had to sell."

"Why to Discovery? This place will go down the tubes!" Sterling felt bad as soon as he said that, he knew Cliff did not need the pressure of the company's problems on top of his family obligations.

"They were the first to meet my offer and they paid already. Surprisingly, I know, but what the hell else was I suppose do to Sterling? I hate doing this to the writers, but I have a little boy to think about."

Just then, Cliff's assistant, Jessica came through the door with a cartload of flowers.

"Delivery for you, Mr. Ardent." She left the cart aside his desk and left the office.

"What the hell?" Clifford reached in for a card and grimaced as soon as he saw the handwriting. Hell, at least she took the time to write the damn card herself. He opened it and chuckled and threw it on the desk, causing Sterling's interest to rise as he grabbed it and read: *So sorry about your son. If there is anything I can do, please do call me, Clifford. Good luck with everything in the future. Sincerely, Alexandra Tate.*

Sterling snickered as well. He knew just from talks with Cliff that he and Alexandra were archrivals in the publishing world. He heard that she was an icy cold bitch and no one dared cross her path but he had never had the pleasure to meet with her.

"Imagine that. She has a heart after all," Sterling said.

Cliff looked up at him. "I have been meaning to talk to you about this, Sterling. You need a publisher and I will not let Discovery ruin you, and I think you know better as well."

"What are you getting at, Cliff?"

"You need to get your manuscripts over to Tate."

Sterling just sat and stared at Cliff. He wanted him to go work for their rival. "I don't understand, Cliff. You hate that woman."

"I know but I have personal reasons for hating the bitch. You don't. She is good, Sterling. Why do you think we have been in competition with her for the last ten years?"

"I don't know, Cliff. I will have to think about it." Sterling started to get up. Cliff stopped him and looked him straight in the eye.

"Sterling, if anyone can make you famous, it is Alexandra Tate."

The boardroom was buzzing with whispers as Alexandra floated into the room. As soon as she walked in, it went dead silent. You could have heard a pin drop. She stopped at the head of the table and wished everyone a good morning. The looks on their faces amused her. She had them all scared out of their wits, every single one of them waiting to be fired or something even worse, like getting scolded in front of the whole company. That was one reason Alex figured her employees were so loyal to her. Not only were they paid extremely well with full benefits she paid for, but they were also under her ever-watchful eye and if they dared cross her, she embarrassed them in front of everyone. In the last ten years, only one person has ever had the balls to test her limits and he suffered the consequences. She smiled as she thought of the day she fired Clifford Ardent, getting him so angry, he went off and started his own company. He made the mistake of being a bit too friendly with her in front of staff and guests. She let him know he had made a mistake.

"Good morning, everyone. I can see you are all a bit tense this morning so before I give you the good news, you can all relax, no one is getting fired here today." She chuckled to herself as most of the people in the room slouched just a bit more and released the tension.

"I got a phone call this morning that brought music to my ears. As you all know, we have been in stiff competition with Ardent Publishing for about ten years, since Tate was started. This morning, Clifford Ardent sold his company to Discovery Printing." She gave everyone a minute to soak it in and talk amongst themselves over the surprising news. She held her hand up and everyone was silent again.

"Over a hundred authors will be looking for new places to publish, as I have already heard that very few of them will be staying with Discovery. That means each and every one of you has a job to do in the next two weeks. One single word. Recruitment! I want as many of those authors to sign with us as possible, I know Mr. Ardent had a good eye for writers and they are all well qualified to write for Tate. I have one special request." Everyone's ears perked up. "Whoever brings me Sterling Morris—don't worry about getting him to sign, I will handle that—whoever brings me Mr. Morris will get a fat bonus in their check and a paid week off. That will be all, people. Lunch will be brought in for you all today to celebrate the good news. Everyone enjoy."

Alex picked up her materials and walked out, knowing fully well that everyone was talking now, and staring at her, trying to comprehend the unbelievable news they just heard. She did love her employees and it made her feel good to treat them. She smiled all the way back to her office. She would have Sterling Morris, in her company writing away bestsellers, and in her bedroom.

THREE

Jackson and Celia Ripley were sitting at their usual table at Champagne Charlie's, the most popular restaurant in downtown Milwaukee. Celia was on her cellphone, as usual, going over appointments and talking to suppliers about new products for the salon. Her nails and hair were perfectly sculpted as usual. Jack was reading his Saturday paper and sipping his Bloody Marys, as he was accustomed to every Saturday morning. Champagne Charlie's specialized in their "all you can eat" brunches on the weekends, which consisted of food fit for a king, and all the free champagne you can drink, of course. Celia was an expert at diving into that treat, as Jack hated the stuff, and stuck to his Bloody Marys or screwdrivers.

Celia clicked off her phone and looked at her husband and at her watch.
"Where is this friend of yours, Sterling, Jack? Is he always late? And how come I have not met him before today?"

"Celia, darling, you have met him, at one of his book signings I took you to, but you were too busy making appointments with people you knew to even bother his existence. And he called me to say he would be a few minutes late." As soon as Celia rolled her eyes and picked up her cellphone again, Sterling walked in the door. He spotted his friend and his upscale wife and walked over to them. He leaned over and gave Celia a peck on the check. She sweetly smiled and kept on talking.

"Always a pleasure, Celia. Jackson, how are you this fine morning." He shook his friend's hand and sat down.

"Same shit, different day, Sterling. How is the hunt for the publisher going?"

"Christ, I have had about twenty phone calls from Tate Publishing this morning alone! I think Alex Tate has an agenda!" Celia quick looked up from her phone call thinking she heard a name she recognized and then went back to her phone.

Sterling ordered a screwdriver and excused himself to go grab a plate. "Holy shit, Jack, you didn't tell me there would be this much food here."

"I told you to bring your appetite, Sterling." Sterling walked over to the first set up in the huge room full of decorated buffets and tables of fine foods.

The seafood bar, he has hit gold right away. He stood there for a moment to admire the set up. On top of the mountains of ice was an array of fresh New England lobster, Alaskan King Crab, Louisiana White Shrimp, fresh caviar, Snow Creek and Willipa Bays raw oysters, and a huge King Salmon fillet, smoked to perfection. Sterling dug in, as he was actually famished this morning, and filled his plate with the delicacies. Jacks eyes popped right open when he saw Sterling's plate piled high.

"Hungry, Sterling, old boy?" Jack laughed. "You will need your strength talking to that Tate bitch!" The two men started laughing until they caught Celia's glare.

"Are you referring to Alex Tate?" she asked coldly.

"Yes, hon, but why would you possibly be concerned about Alexandra Tate, the ice queen of the publishing world?" The guys were still laughing.

"Jackson Ripley, do you ever listen to anything I say? Do you remember my telling you about some high-priced clients I had that we make special arrangements for and actually travel to them with our services? Alexandra Tate is one of my biggest clients and a very good friend of mine! I would appreciate you both cut with the name calling!" The men just stared at each other and then at Celia.

"You mean to tell me you are friends with that woman?" Jackson guffawed.

"Jack, she is not like everyone says. She is really a nice person, she just knows how to handle her business." Sterling stepped in on that note.

"Yes, like firing Cliff Ardent in front of God and everyone. That wasn't crude now, was it?" Sterling elbowed Jack and they started talking about the infamous event. Celia stood up with her purse and appointment book.

"Jack, really! I refuse to sit here with you while you and your friend bash my friends to pieces! Grow up, will you! Sterling, I apologize; it was nice to have met you. Good day to you both." She put on her Ralph Lauren sunglasses and stomped out of the restaurant.

"Sorry, Jack. Did not mean to get you into trouble."

"Sterling! Do you realize what that means? You can get into Tate Publishing today if you wanted. I can go home, kiss the wife's ass a little and have her call Alex for us. What do you say? Your book is not writing itself you know, you need to get into a company and fast."

"Hell no, Jack. Dammit, I am standing by Cliff's side. He wants me to go over there, too. After the way she treated him, hell no. She can rot in hell for all I care. She is NOT getting my ass in her company."

"Maybe it isn't your ass I want, Mr. Morris." Sterling and Jackson looked up from their conversation to find Alexandra Tate standing at their table. Both of them were speechless, first from the interruption and surprise at their guest and second, at the astounding beauty of her.

"May I join you?" Alex asked as she took her friend's place at the table. Sterling stood up in the gentleman like manner he was accustomed to.

"Of course. Miss Tate, I presume?" Sterling sat back down, not taking an eye off the vixen in front of him. His guard was up still, not knowing if all the rumors were true or not.

"You presume correct, Mr. Morris. And you must be Celia's husband, Jackson Ripley." She shook hands with both of them and ordered herself a stiff vodka martini.

"I am in town on personal business with your wife actually, Jackson. I received a phone call not ten minutes ago from Celia, a bit hysterical I must say for her, letting me know of your whereabouts and of your conversation." She stopped there waiting for the reaction that she expected. Both men put their heads down in embarrassment from being caught at calling Alex what they thought she was.

"Please, do not be embarrassed on my account. I know the rumors about me. They do not bother me at all. I did not come here to talk business Mr. Morris. I came here just to introduce myself and finally meet you. Here is my card. Do call me. We can meet for lunch sometime, my town or yours. Now, if you boys will excuse me, I have to catch up with dear Celia and then run off to the airport to catch my flight home. Nice chatting with you both." She got up and left them, not touching her martini, not letting either one of them speak. They both sat there for a moment in silence until Jack finally spoke.

"What was that about, Sterling?" Jack asked, looking for some explanation at the odd meeting that happened just now.

"That was the character in my next book, Jack. Hahaha. Did you see how perfect she looked? You could melt ice on that ass of hers!" Sterling was wide-eyed and full of ideas running through his head. "Don't worry old chap, I am not giving in to her, but I am writing her in my book. I have to go, thoughts don't stay around too much these days!" Sterling got up and dashed out the door, leaving Jackson there confused as ever.

As Sterling Morris ran out of Champagne Charlie's, Alexandra Tate sat in her limo down the street watching carefully. He was the opposite of what she had imagined, or had hoped for. She thought of his books and wanted to live them out with whoever wrote them and was hoping for a stallion, a Greek God, and what she found was Ichabod Crane, a tall lanky fellow with a big nose and long fingers. She smiled, thinking possibly, just maybe, there may be something to this man. She watched him dash to his Monte Carlo and drive off quickly. She knocked on the glass window separating her and her driver, letting him know she was ready to go. She picked up her cellphone and dialed a number.

"Celia my darling, thank you so much for that little tidbit of info you gave me. I think I made quite an impression on our Mr. Morris. Now, we must discuss details of this dinner party at my house. Remember, you must convince Jackson to come and to bring Sterling with him, although they will both be invited." A pause. "What was that darling? Of course! Why else would I invite him to my house!" Alex laughed all the way to the airport.

FOUR

Angeline Frost came walking out of the private dressing room of the exclusive, very expensive upscale fashion shop, wearing a pair of designer high heel shoes and holding a dress on a satin covered hanger straight to either side. Her gray eyes were literally sending out sparks as she frowned down at the cute, petite sales associate with short curly hair.

Angeline always insisted on being nude at any time she was trying on clothes or having her selections fitted. That way, she could always select the most correct and gossamer undergarments to complete the illusion she was nude under any outfit she chose to wear.

"Vicki, I personally stood a good fifteen Goddamned minutes while your seamstress marked these dresses for alterations." Angeline raised the dresses higher. "Can you please tell me why the fuck these dresses are so far above my knee my bald headed, sawed-off little fucker of a boss could see my cunt sitting right off on the end of his nose?"

Her first impulse was to laugh uproariously at the funny picture her words

29

had painted on the screen of her mind. The urge died as her eyes began to move up Angeline's absolutely perfectly shaped and proportioned legs which was very unusual since Angeline stood five-feet eleven inches tall in stocking feet. Her eyes lingered of their own accord on the curly black triangle of soft, curly, black pubic hair and followed the point all the way between her legs, contrasting so beautifully with her pale, alabaster skin she carefully protected from the sun since no amount of sun screen would protect her from burning to the point she had to seek medical attention.

Vicki was forced to lick her lips as her gaze traveled up her athletic torso, briefly hesitating on her large conical breasts with perfectly matched pink, pointed nipples before searching for her almost unbelievably beautiful face ringed by her perfectly cut and styled hair, accentuated by the natural color of her lips that seldom needed any artificial color to be just right for any occasion.

Tilting her head to one side, Vicki silently vowed she would kill or die for one night in bed with her. She was an avowed lesbian and Angeline Frost came closer to the mental picture she had of the ideal woman than any female she had ever had the opportunity to admire completely nude. Unfortunately, her ideal woman was just as much an avowed heterosexual. Even worse, her hairdresser, a real hunk and a bisexual, had been to bed with her. Ricky said Angeline gave the best blowjob he had ever experienced. When she questioned him severely, he admitted several men had come close, but she still held the loving cup. She was somewhat appeased when he admitted several men and one other female could out-fuck her, but made her mad when he said the female was as ugly as a painted baboon.

"Miss Frost," Vicki said, taking a step toward her with a concerned expression, "I don't have slightest idea why your clothes don't fit perfectly. They always do."

"Not this time," Angeline said, dropping the hangers and turning to one side. "And the next time I'm called away from my desk at a very busy New York brokerage firm where I happen to be the only female employed there and taller than most of the men, forcing me to fight for my very existence every hour of every day, they sure as hell better be perfect. If they're not, I'll take all my business away from this shitty little fashion shop."

Ann Botts, the store manager, stood by Vicki as they watched Angeline disappear past the plate glass window.

"You can forget about the 'ice princess', Vicki."

"Why, do you know something I don't?"

"Yeah, I tried for three years before you got here to bed the bitch with no success."

Vicki laughed. "Well, you can't blame a guy for trying."

"You're right, but don't forget THE MONKEY'S PAW."

"I don't get your drift."

"If you're not careful, you might get what you wish for."

"Would that be so bad?"

"In Angeline's case, that ice cave she calls a mouth would try to freeze you to death, and you don't have a big enough dick to shove in there to choke the snow blower."

They laughed before turning their attention to three new customers, coming in the glass doors.

Sterling cracked his knuckles loudly and sat back in his leather chair with a satisfied smile on his face as if he had just given a woman the best orgasm she had ever had. He wanted to write about Alexandra Tate and her perfectly sculpted body, salon perfect hair and delicately painted lips. He wanted to live out the moments with her. He chuckled at the thought. Can you imagine? Alexandra Tate is giving him, the birdman, a second chance? Sterling had only been with one other woman his whole life, back in high school. He still considered himself a virgin. The girls at school made fun of him because his arms were too long, he was all legs and his nose was too big. The one girl he did have sex with moved away before they could get into a serious relationship. She'd told him he was the best lover she had ever had. That was when he started writing. He wrote about all of the wonderful things he wanted to do to women. He closed his eyes and fell into a daydream.

Alexandra Tate was sitting in his office, waiting for him. They were to meet and talk about his upcoming book and her possibly publishing it for him. She sat on the leather couch with her legs crossed and her high heels pointed to the sky. When Sterling walked in, she stood and shook his hand, commenting on how the pleasure was all hers to come this far. Sterling eyed her up as she sat back down. She had on a navy suit consisting of no more than a short pinstriped skirt and a matching blazer. He was positive there was nothing under either one of them. She caught him looking and uncrossed her legs slowly. She asked him if there was anything else he was interested in discussing. Sterling walked over to the door and locked it. When he turned around, Alexandra had her buttons undone on her blazer and just as he had suspected, there was nothing underneath except two beautiful milky white breasts with large succulent light brown nipples. They perked right out and begged him for attention. He walked over to her, not paying the least bit of attention to the enormous bulge in his trousers. Alexandra caught site of it, though, and her eyes grew in amazement. He really was everything she had imagined. Sterling grabbed her by the shoulders and kissed her hard and passionately. Alexandra's knees went weak and she fell back onto the couch. Sterling held onto her all the way down and knelt in front of her. He looked up and grinned. This was the part he loved so much. He hiked up her skirt and spread her legs wide. There in front of him was a perfect little triangle of raven black curls. He decided not to be gentle today. The romantic lover would have to wait; today he wanted to be the barbarian. His tongue dove in as Alexandra flew off the couch. He held her down and dug in further. When the bridge of his enormous nose rubbed on her clitoris, her juices started flowing like the Amazon between her thighs. He lapped it up and savored the moment. Alex sat there in wide-eyed amazement as Sterling stood and unbuckled his pants. When they dropped in front of her, she sat up, ready to

receive whatever he had in store for her. When she saw it, she gasped. That explained the big nose. It was just massive. She smiled and wrapped her long candy red polished nails around the shaft…

"Sterling!" Sterling jumped in his chair back into reality. His publicist, Anne Marie, was yelling at him from the door. He nearly jumped up until he realized what a site it would be when she saw the front of his pants bulging out like that. *What has gotten into him?*

"Yes, Anne Marie? Sorry, I was daydreaming."

"Miss Tate is on line one for you, sir." Anne Marie closed his door and left him staring at the phone. He was not sure what to say to her but he picked up the receiver and placed it close to his ear.

"Hello, Miss Tate?"

"Sterling! I am so glad I caught you! I do apologize if I am interrupting anything dear. I just wanted to apologize for my abruptness at lunch today. I did not mean to seem so short with you."

"Nonsense, Miss Tate…" Alexandra cut him off.

"Oh please, Sterling, call me Alexandra. All my friends do." So that was it…they were friends now?

"I was actually just thinking of you, Miss Ta…uh, Alexandra."

"Really? And what on earth for, Sterling? Do tell." *If you only knew, lady. If you only knew.*

"I was just thinking that it was nice to finally meet you. I have heard so much about you from Clifford."

"Ah yes, Mr. Advent. That really is tragic about Clifford's little boy, isn't it? I hope he gets well and makes it through everything all right. My heart goes out to both of them." Sterling was just not sure how to take Alexandra yet. Cliff made it sound like she was the devil in disguise yet

Sterling had seen nothing but politeness. And Cliff failed to mention she was hot as hell.

"Yes, well, they have the best doctors, so hopefully, Justin won't go through too much torture. Was there a reason you called, Miss Tate?"

"Alex, Sterling, really. There is no need to be so formal, is there? I was calling to see if you had any plans on the 21st. I am throwing a rather extravagant party at my house for my authors and potential new clients. I would love for you and the Ripleys to be there."

"Are you inviting me to come and write for your company, Miss Tate?"
Sterling was on guard now. She was playing her cards and he could feel the Ace slipping by him.
"Oh, that's all business, Sterling. I would like for you to come and meet other authors, mingle, get to know folks from the big publishing world."

From the rich and glamorous, you mean, Sterling thought.

"I will see what I can do, Alexandra. It sounds like fun."

"Wonderful, Sterling, just wonderful! The invitations are going out today. Promise you will be there and I promise, no talk of business."

"All right, Alex, I will be there, but only if Jack tags along."

"Oh, of course, Celia has already made the commitment!" *That doesn't mean her husband has*. Sterling rolled his eyes. Celia always had commitments.

"I will see you then, Alexandra."

"Ciao for now then, Mr. Morris. Until we meet again." There was a loud click and she was gone. *That woman has something up her sleeve. Or up her skirt…*He turned to the window and picked up in his daydream where he left off, right where he was about to feed the bitch.

Alexandra Tate hung up the phone and sat back in her seat. She was in flight, on her way back to Jackson. She loved teasing people. She loved being the object of their questions. She knew she had Mr. Morris interested, she just needed to hook him in. She hired a planner for the party to get all the arrangements set up. Dealing with all that business was just too much commotion for her. The planner was Julia. She was a beautiful auburn-haired vixen with a nose for organization like she had never seen. She snapped her fingers and they all jumped. She owned her own wedding planning company. They did all kinds of events from weddings to Bar Mitzvahs to extravagant parties like the one Alex was throwing. She gathered from Sterling's plate at Champagne Charlie's that he loved seafood so she was having just tons of it flown in fresh the day of the party from the East Coast. Sterling loved it. She needed to find out what he drank in the evenings. She would sic Celia on that task. Her phone rang. It was Julia.

"Julia, darling, how are you? How are the arrangements coming along?"

"Great, Miss Tate. You said you had some last minute requests to add?"

"Ahh, yes. I will need a limo sent to the airport to pick up Mr. Morris and the Ripleys. I am not sure of the time yet but have one on standby, will you please? I would also like guestrooms prepared for them. One for Mr. Morris and one for the Ripley's. They will all be staying over. Make sure Mr. Morris's room is on the second floor."

"Aren't all the guest rooms on the first floor, ma'am?"

"Yes, dear, but Mr. Morris is a special guest, Julia. He will need extra special attention."

"I see. I will make sure it is done. Anything else?"

"I think that is it for now, Julia. If I can think of anything else, I will call you. Thank you dear!." She hung up the phone again. She smiled, thinking how nice it would be for THE Sterling Morris to have a bedroom on the second floor, right next to her own…

FIVE

Alexandra sat at her desk and stared at all the paperwork she had to do. She loathed paperwork but it needed to be done. She had a stack of mail that was sky high and tons of submissions that were accepted she had to approve. It was definitely Monday. She had been in good spirits ever since she left Mr. Morris in the little metropolis of Milwaukee. He was quite a charmer, she had decided, and planned to go ahead with her next move. She was bound and determined for him to be a major part in their company but she needed to win him over in other ways first. She sorted through the mail and stopped at two envelopes. They were reply cards for her party, both with a Milwaukee, Wisconsin postmark on them. She opened them up as quickly as her sculpted nails allowed her. Her heart skipped a beat when she saw they were from the Ripleys and Sterling Morris. They were all attending. She was delighted and relieved, now that she had the confirmation. She phoned Julia quickly just to let her know of the confirmation. She was not sure what Sterling would think of staying in the same hallway as her so she decided to put the Ripleys there as well. At least that way he would not freak out.

She started thinking about the party. The music was all lined up, the caterers, the decorators, and the hired help. There was no way she was lifting a damn finger that night. She was going to play the hostess and just mingle. She hired butlers, valets, and servers. It was good to be rich, she decided. She wanted Sterling to be a part of that with her. She grinned as she thought of the last passage she had read in his book, *Summer Rain*. She was nearly finished now. That book was responsible for countless nights of self-pleasure, the last being just out of this world. Alex was in her huge round bathtub full of bubbles, reading her book and sipping on a martini. She decided the hell with the drink and had let her fingers find their way deep into the waters below until they discovered a different wetness. She plunged into herself and nearly dropped the book right into the water. Her back was arched damn near right over the edge of the tub. Her fingers were thrashing about wildly and she moaned so loudly, she actually took the time to thank God she had no one in the house with her at night. When she finally came she knocked her martini glass right off the edge of the tub. She did not stop there.

The orgasm was so intense she just could not let her fingers go. She reached down on the floor next to the tub and grabbed a silver vibrator. The Silver Bullet it was called and it was her favorite toy. She inserted it carefully and started thrashing away again until she came twice, then a third time. She had to have this man who wrote with such sexual intensity. By the time she was finished, Alex was exhausted. She rested for about half an hour before she decided to get out and clean the bathroom up, noticing that she had splashed bubbles all over the floor, as well as the broken glass from her martini.

Alex snapped back into reality, noting full well that she was as horny as ever right now. Her silk panties were soaked. She smiled and yelled for whoever was pounding on the door to come in. It was her secretary, Madison. Alex admired Madison Stellmacher. She was a younger version of herself. She was drop dead gorgeous, smart as hell and had a great head for business. She had been Alex's Executive Assistant since she started the company in Jackson. She had a beautiful southern drawl on her that made the boys go wild.

"Madison, sweetie, come on in. You are coming to my party, aren't you? I will not take no for an answer."

"'Course, Alex. I wouldn't dream of missin' it."

"Good, there will be a lot of young single men there." Alex smiled viciously as she watched Madison put her head down and blush. She was still as naive as ever when it came to men. Alex meant to help her change all that. She saw that she was embarrassing her and quickly changed the subject.

"What can I do for you, Madison?" Alex asked as she leaned back in her chair.

Madison approached her desk with an armful of submissions. She looked at Alexandra with a careful eye. She knew this was going to piss her off.

"Well, Arnold left for vacation Friday and these were all found on his desk. They are the submissions that were due to be approved two weeks ago. He ain't touched em, Alex." Alexandra's face went bright red.

"He what?! Why in the hell would he do that?! Christ I can't even yell at the fat little bastard! Son-of-a-bitch! Who else is working in submissions this week?"

"Gloria, Amee, Richard, and Susan. They all have stacks up to their foreheads, Alex. They would have to work overtime to get these done." Madison was the only person in the company that was not afraid of Alex because she knew the other side of her. She knew the nasty bitch was just a front so people would not push her over like they did her father.

"Fuck! Why does this always happen when I am swamped up to my fucking ears? They know I want that deadline met before they step one foot out of the doors on Fridays! Why in the hell would he pull something like this? I swear I will have his balls for breakfast when he comes back! Find out where he went just so I can make his vacation miserable."

Madison looked down at the piles and then back to Alex. "If you don't mind, Alex, I can take a bunch of them home and divide the rest up into the others in submissions."

Alex looked up at Madison; grateful the girl was so bold and grateful for the offer to take the workload. "Are you sure, Madison? I know you have done submissions with me before but there are a lot there!"

"It's no bother, really, Alex. I have nothing to do tonight anyhow." Madison shuffled them all around in her hands and prepared to walk out of the office when Alex jumped up and grabbed her arm.

"You are an angel, Madison! Thank you so much. I will deal with Arnold when the little fucker gets back. Can you send Amee in here right away too, please? Thank you darling." Alex dismissed her just like that, as she usually did at the end of her conversations and waited for Amee to get there.

She arrived not five minutes later, always punctual, that girl. She was blonde and very petite, about 5' 2" tall. Very cute, Alex noted. She knocked as Alex waved her in and told her to have a seat. Amee looked petrified.

"Calm down, Amee. I did not ask you here to yell at you. I am going to be very blunt." Amee was still prepared for the worst. She hated it when Miss Tate said that. "How would you like to be the new Head of Submissions?" She waited as Amee's eyed bugged out and then she looked at Alex as if she was crazy and then let the shock set in.

"Take your time, Amee. This is a big decision. But after Arnold's negligence this weekend, I just cannot allow that to happen any longer. You will get a raise to go along with the other benefits that come with the position. You will have to start immediately though, making sure all the deadlines get met for this week." Amee damn near jumped onto Alex's desk.

"Of course, Miss Tate! Thank you! Thank you so much! You don't know what this means! Oh, I just don't..."

"All right for Christ's sake, girl! Don't have an orgasm!" Alex interrupted. Amee blushed at her sexual comment. Alex excused her and quickly buzzed Madison to have her draw up the new papers.

Madison arrived at her apartment in Humboldt, TN at seven pm. She was used to the long hours, always cleaning up Alex's paperwork she never finished. She never minded. Alex paid her more than anyone did in the company, even the department heads. She was worth it all. Her apartment was very upscale, like that of Alexandra Tate's house. She loved her boss's house and tried to mimic her style. Her carpets were plush, her furniture leather. She dropped the stack of submissions on the oak roll-top desk in her study. She knew it was going to be a long night so she changed in to something more comfortable and pulled a bottle of wine from the refrigerator. Fuck the glass, she decided, I am drinking right out of the damn bottle.

After about two hours of reading and tossing things into about four different piles, there was a knock on the door. Madison was relieved for the break. She opened the door and stood there shocked to see Alex Tate standing before her, a bottle of wine in hand. She was dressed casually, in jeans and a silk blouse. Her leather sandals wrapped her perfectly little feet. Madison could not find words except to find out what the hell she wanted.

"Alex, wh...what are you doin' here?" Madison opened the door further to let her boss in. Alex waltzed right in like she was an invited guest.

"I felt just awful after letting you take all that work so I decided to come over and help." Madison closed the door and stood there. She could not believe it. Her boss, help someone? "Madison, your apartment is exquisite. I love your taste darling."

"That really isn't necessary, Alex. I have it all under control."

"Nonsense," Alex dismissed her comment with the wave of a hand. "This is too damn much reading for one person and I need you bright eyed and bushy tailed for me tomorrow. I have meetings all day long." Madison reached to the cupboards and got her boss a wineglass. She felt Alex's eyes scouting the length of her fit body in her tight little shorts she had on. She blew it off. She had always suspected Alex to be a player, and quite frankly wouldn't mind playing with her but quickly dismissed the ideas.

"Thank you, darling. You are such a dear." Alex scanned the ground looking at all of the materials Madison was going over. "You have been such a busy little girl. Let's get busy. The sooner we get this all done, the sooner we can sit and chat."

Two hours and two bottles of Merlot later, the girls were giggling out loud with each other, making fun of this author or that, a few choice words. They finally both got into a book they could not get out of. It was by an author by the name of Thomas Moore Williams. Odd, they both thought, neither of them had heard of this one. They continued to read.

Frank Dark stood at rear of the upper deck of the yacht, watching Mary Leigh Bulcher park her car. He glanced at his watch and smiled. She was right on time.

Mary Leigh she got out of her little pink convertible and modestly straightened her tight, form-fitting skirt before looking around to get her bearing. As she walked to the guardhouse to get clearance to THE GETAWAY, a beautiful one-hundred-and-fifteen-foot Gulf Breeze Mariner

owned by her boss, Frank couldn't help but think her gorgeous, well-formed legs were perfect to his way of thinking. Feet on one end and pussy on the other.

Most men who came though the front office where she worked chose to ignore Mary Leigh because she took her job seriously, never joked or flirted, and always acted in a professional manner. Frank reached down and stroked his semi-hard, congratulating himself on his astute observation there was more to her than anyone had ever dared to guess.

Mary Leigh captured Frank's full attention when she was leaned over filing cabinet with her back to him, allowing him the opportunity to access her legs from her ankles to well past her knees. Frank immediately knew from the promise he saw in front of him, she would be a prize indeed gracing any bed, posing in the nude, even if she had no tits at all. By the time she raised up and turned around, he was going into David's office, but not before he made himself promise to get to know her better.

Her boss was David Cupper, who had become rich in the banking business after he graduated from college with honors with a major in finance. David was extremely smart, but was lacking in common sense. By the time he met Frank, David had a lot of toys and plenty of money to replace those he had broken because he liked to play rough.

Frank met David on a skeet-shooting range. David struck up a conversation when Frank hit every target with very basic equipment; while David hit one out of a possible twenty with the best money could buy. After more than several drinks in popular, rundown, hole in the wall bar, they had become acquainted.

Within a week, they were close friends. They found what they were missing in each other. Frank was a consummate male. Dark, handsome and athletic with natural ability to excel in just about anything he undertook, but he lacked one basic ingredient to become a real man of the world. Frank had no steady job, no money in the bank, and no resources he could call on. As a result, he was always on the outside looking in at the society in which he so much wanted to be a player.

David on the other hand, had all the money and the right connections, but was a fish out of water outside a bank or in a financial atmosphere. But with Frank by his side to guide him, he was able to finally blend in with the beautiful people who were constantly swirling around him, leaving him dizzy trying to keep up with them as they flitted hither and yon.

Frank proved to be the catalyst between the two of them. David had the money while Frank had the absolute know how. Most of the time, all David had to do was point Frank in the right direction and tag along. Within a short time, they had become known as the "Goodtime Boys," cutting a swath anywhere and everywhere, trampling over anyone, man or woman, who dared to stand in their way.

On a Friday morning, David called Frank to his office to tell him why they had to cancel their weekend plans. He was being called out of town on a pressing banking problem in another state. David asked Frank if he would mind straightening out some wearisome deficits on THE GETAWAY that had perplexed the maintenance crew since he didn't have time to take the yacht to the shipyard and get it back before an *important party for a group of banking executives were coming in from around the country for promised weekend of fishing, fucking and fun.*

Frank had studied the list and almost told David he could take care everything he wanted done in a day. Dropping the list from in front of his face, Mary Leigh has come walking by David's office window, stopped, leaned over, pulled her dress up slightly, and pretended to be straightening her pantyhose while she looked up at Frank with a promise in her sparkling green eyes. Following a wink to let her know the message was well understood; Frank turned to David and told him the work would be no real problem, but to get it all done, he would need to spend the whole weekend on board. Relieved, David quickly agreed and gave him an electronic key to everything aboard.

On his way out, Frank had stopped by Mary Leigh's desk. Using a relaxed posture and quiet voice, he had invited her to join him for a drink and dinner on board when she got off work. Looking up, the professional smile never left her face as she not only agreed, but also informed him that she was taking off two hours early.

Frank stood by the short gangplank with his hand on the rope, watching Mary Leigh coming toward him. He couldn't help but wonder if the wonderful shade of her auburn hair was natural, because if it were, her pussy would shine like a rare jewel in the soft glow of the ships lights. Having been with his share of redheads, he had a clear idea as to what covered the entrance to their honey walls, but pussy hair the color of the hair on her head would be a new and wonderful experience. As she was approaching with her arms held out to him, he glanced down was immediately mortified. His pleasant introspection had given him a rigid hard-on, sticking out of the front of his pants.

Before he could react, Mary Leigh had gone up on her tiptoes, thrown her arms around his neck, thrown her hips forward, pulled his head down and crushed their lips together his while her tongue explored his tonsils. Frank was immediately surprised. He had experienced many kisses in his time, but never had one taken his breath away.

Mary Leigh lay back in his arms and smiled up at him. "Is that a boat tool in your pocket, sailor, or are you just happy to see me."

Frank smiled his appreciation. "I'd like to say it's a gut wrench. But after that kiss, I'm not really sure."

"Well," she said, taking his hand and pulling him up the gangplank,

"we'll never know standing out here talking will we?"

Frank allowed her to think she was pulling him along. "What would you suggest?"

"Find the nearest cabin, get naked and hit the bed where you can bury your face in my pussy while I suck your dick."

"What about the drink?"

"Tell hell with the drink. I been watching and wanting you for so long I'd fuck you right here on the gangplank if that is your desire."

Frank rushed in front, pulling her instead to lead the way, ducking in the first guest cabin they came to. There was only enough room for them to stand on either side of the bed and watch other undress, adding to the lust threatening to consume them before they could quench the roaring flame.

When he pulled her labia wide apart and began to run his tongue up one side and down the other before going up the middle and around her clitoris, she began to moan. Encouraged, he brought his fingers into play, darting in and out and all around of her vagina.

"Oh my God," she screamed, "I knew you'd be good! But not this fucking good! Hell, I cum-m-m-m-ming!"

Frank waited until the spasms had stopped before he slowed his action, moving his attention to her whole body. Making sure every erogenous zone had been given his full attention.

Mary Leigh finally wiggled out from under him, and looking directly into the eyes, she smiled at the question she found there. "It's your turn now, and I'm going to try and give you every bit as good as you've given me."

"I've only done what I always do. It wasn't anything special."
Scooting off the end of the bed, she took his feet and spread them wide "If that's true, I've wasted one hell of a time by not meeting you before now."

"Don't worry," Frank said, his breath coming in short breaths as her tongue began running up his leg, quickly approaching his balls, leaving a trail of pleasure every inch

of the way, "I plan to repeat what I did over and over again until you have to leave."

"When do you have to get off this wonderful yacht I've been trying to get on since Mr. Cupping acquired it in a hostile takeover?"

"Sometime Sunday afternoon," he groaned, "I'm having dinner with David at his mansion."

Mary Leigh was pleased, watching the pain of pleasure progress across his handsome features, moving her hands up and down in opposite directions, letting go and tickling on his balls on the downstroke. "Well, mister sailor," she said before taking him in her mouth and fully down her throat, "we've got lots and lots of fucking to do. So we'd better get at it."

When he began to thrust his hips up and down and she knew he was ready to orgasm, she slid up and over him, inserting his jerking organ into her wet, hairy welcomes where they jerked and trembled for almost a full minute.

When Frank was almost spent and started to pullout, she raised her hips.
"Don't pull you dick out yet. It's still stiff enough for me to get my nuts one more time."

She buried her face in his neck and began to move her hips in earnest. In spite of himself, Frank found new life and managed to stay inside her until she was ready to go yet another time.

Mary Leigh leaned on the doorjamb completely nude, watching him concentrate on rewiring a faulty circuit. Frank had gotten up early, but left her to sleep. When she was fully awake, she found a note on his pillow. He had fixed her a large and healthy breakfast, citing how hungry she was after they had been making love to the wee hours before they took a shower together before getting in bed to sleep.

Watching until she thought he was too cute for words, Mary Leigh walked over, threw her arms around him and kissed him between his broad shoulders while she thrust her mons venus between his buttocks.

"You are such a darling man."

"You may be fight about you observation, ma'am." Frank said and laughed, looking over his shoulder. "But I promised your boss I'd get some work done around here."

"Are you saying that I'm keeping you from your work?"

Frank turned to face her with a tool held in each hand out to either side. "Damn right you are!"

Mary Leigh unzipped his shorts and went down on her knees in front of him. Before she could carry out her intention, Frank went down on his knees and put his hands gently on her shoulders. Pushing her down on her back, he pulled her knees over his shoulders.

"Me first. I couldn't see you the way I wanted too in the cabin. There a full light coming through the portholes in here, and this time, I want to get a clear enough mental picture to last me a lifetime. I may never see a pussy as prettier as yours ever again."

"In that case, sir," Mary Leigh said and giggled, spreading her legs apart, "look, feel, and lick to you hearts content. Just don't forget to fuck me before you're through down there. I've never had a dick like yours in me before."

Looking up through her auburn pubic hair with a wicked grin, Frank said,

"We if keep this up all weekend, I'll never get through."
Mary Leigh grinned right back. "Not even the list of things my boss asked you to do."

They both laughed until his tongue began to go around and around her anus before traveling the wet path between her soft, pink labia which contrasted so wonderfully with the auburn pubic air. Mary Leigh didn't have enough breath to laugh and Frank was concentrating on what he was doing.

So the time went with them making love all over the yacht, oblivious to the maintenance crew who had seen it all before, time and time again. To satisfy all their goals, Mary Leigh resorted to putting a tool belt on and helping him whenever she could.

As all good things do, the weekend came to an end with them standing on the dock next to the short gangplank. Following a long, meaningful goodbye kiss, Mary Leigh looked into his eyes. "Hey, sailor, you wouldn't have time for me to suck your dick one more time would you?"

Frank grabbed her hand and began pulling her up the gangplank with one hand, rubbing his crotch with the other. "Heaven would have to wait for that!"

By the time they had gotten that far, Alex was wet between the legs and she could see that Madison was worked up as well. She put her glass down and leaned over to Madison. Her little assistant was going to comment but Alex put a finger to her lips, shushing her. She reached under Madison's shirt and squeezed a firm breast. Madison gasped and grabbed Alex by the back of the head and kissed her forcefully but passionately. Her aggressiveness shocked Alex but she did not pull away. Her hand found Alex's breasts and she played with her perfect nipples until they were both perky as could be. Alex whimpered, Madison moaned. They fell into the pile of papers on top of one another. Madison's shorts were soon undone by an unseen hand. Alex's fingers quickly found their way to Madison's treasure box. Madison moaned loudly and ripped off Alex's jeans. She pushed Alex to the floor and spread her legs. Her face glistened as she licked the flowing juices from her boss's thighs. She shoved her tongue into the pink folds of flesh, grabbing onto her thighs harder so Alex could not move. She fucked Alex's pussy with her tongue until the ice queen melted and came all over Madison's pretty little face. Alex gladly returned the favor to Madison. Madison had never experienced anything like this before. Not with a woman, with anyone's tongue for sure. She was in pure ecstasy. When they were done, they cleaned up the mess, spending another hour sorting out the papers they messed up. They agreed to speak of this to no one and Alex left, bidding Madison a good night and sweet dreams.

SIX

Celia had her best hairdresser do her hair any time she needed to go out. She refused to do it herself, as it was just too much hassle. Her nails were being painted Shimmering Pearl. Her gown for the party was emerald green. Celia was a very beautiful woman, but a beauty that was bought and paid for every month. Included in her $4,000 a month beauty regimen was tanning every week, her hair done every week, manicure and pedicure twice month and the full spa treatment of course. Celia's philosophy was that there just wasn't a price one could put on beauty. It cost whatever it took to look like a supermodel. Except supermodels get away with it a lot easier than that. Celia's dress has cost her just over six grand. She never told her husband what she spent, but always made sure she was out of the house when he was going over the bank statements. He did not mind too much, considering the fact that it was basically her salon they lived off of. Jack's editing made them money off the bigger client's, especially if the books were hits, but not enough to support their lavish lifestyle in the city. She bought Jackson a new tuxedo for the evening. He must have a dozen that have only been worn once to one big event she made him attend at one time or another. To her surprise, he was not complaining about going to Miss Tate's party; partially because he found her fascinating and also because he was trying to get his friend, Sterling Morris, to publish with her. Celia knew Alex had the hots for Sterling and never said a peep to her husband about it, Alex would kill her. She pretended to not know a thing while Alex prepared to go in for the kill.

Sterling had his tuxedo pressed for the party this evening. He was nervous about meeting up with Miss Tate again; she was very forward with him and he was not sure how to take her. She was either being overly friendly, trying to get him to sign with her company or she was just a very flirty young lady and wanted him in the sack. He chuckled at the thought of himself in bed with a vixen like that. In his dreams someday. Alexandra Tate would probably laugh him right out of her house. He was doing rather well at writing her into a book he was working on. She had taken on the identity of a true bitch, an ice queen, just as everyone thought Alex was. Sterling saw right through her. She was just trying to live up to her reputation.

Three hours later, the Ripleys picked up Sterling in their Mercedes and sped off to the airport. Alexandra had paid for the flights as well. Milwaukee to Memphis, first class. Alex's limousine was waiting for them when they got off the plane. Sterling was nervous as hell for some reason. He just could not get it out of his head that little Miss Tate had evil intentions.

Alex glanced around the dining room one last time at the exquisite seafood buffet she had catered in especially for Mr. Morris. There were tables of shaved ice covered with shrimp, lobster, caviar, oysters, clams, mussels, only to name a few of the items. She was quite delighted. Being a replica of one of the oldest plantations in the south, it was massive in space. One room, just adjacent to the dining area was the bar, a full bar and plenty of smaller tables for seating and socializing. In the room beyond that, was the ballroom. There was a live band for the evening's entertainment, already set up. She walked back towards the front entryway, where two butlers stood and a clerk to check the coats. Alex spared no expense.

The first to arrive was Madison, as usual, always punctual. She held her hand out to Alex and they exchanged quick pecks on the cheek. Madison commented on how lovely Alex looked and Alex returned the compliment to young Madison. Madison was wearing a strappy little number from Valentini with three inch high heels from Dolce & Gabbana, The dress was scarlet red and showed quite a bit of skin. Madison did not mind showing off her body. She was young, and single, she kept reminding herself. She just had to tell Alex about finding nearly perfect matching shoes from a completely different designer. Madison and Alex were very up to date on their fashion design. Alex herself was wearing the latest in the Donatello Versace collection. She knew she would be the hit of the party, looking perfect, as she was used to. The Ripleys arrived with Sterling in tow an hour and a half later. Alex fussed over Celia's Galliano dress and the Armani tux she chose for Jackson. She was pleased to see that Sterling was wearing Armani as well. *That must have cost him half his paycheck in royalties, Alex thought. There will be no more of that if he signs with me.* She held out her hand to Sterling, telling him how delighted she was that he could make it. Sterling barely heard a word she said, as the site of her mesmerized him. Her raven hair was flowing freely down her naked back. Her body was hugged by the sapphire blue Versace dress Alex was wearing. Her ears were decorated with sparkling blue sapphires.

Sterling's gaze went to her neck, where a matching sapphire blue necklace adorned her graceful collarbone. He stopped at her face, where her ruby red lips were full and begging to be kissed and her ice blue eyes stood out all the more with the dress. Jackson nudged Sterling and Sterling jumped out of his wicked daydream.

He picked up her hand and kissed it, looking up at her with his amber eyes. "A pleasure, Miss Tate. The devil certainly does wear a blue dress." Alex was flattered by the compliment. Sterling Morris, her favorite author was in her house. She just could not believe it. She took Sterling by the arm and led him and Jackson into the bar for refreshment, leaving Celia to mingle with old friends and clients of hers. Sterling stopped short of the dining room and was overjoyed that he had not eaten yet today.

"Mr. Morris, you don't mind if I am around you too much tonight I hope.
I want to get you used to the crowds, the life. I want you to sign with Tate, Mr. Morris, I am sure you are well aware of that by now." Alex had cut right to the chase. No time to prepare for what he would say at all. Sterling and Jackson looked at each other and then at her.

"Miss Tate," Sterling started.

Alex quickly interrupted him. "Alex, please, Sterling. No need to be so formal among friends now is there?"

"Alex, of course," Sterling continued. " What makes you think I am ready to make that decision yet? I know nothing of your company besides what the public knows."

"I know that, Sterling, but that is all business jargon. Really. We can work something out another day but tonight I want you to let yourself go, cut loose. Have fun! You mustn't be so shy!" She led the men into the dining room and left them there to eat and talk among themselves as gracefully moved back to the front hall to greet more guests.

Sterling had a pissed off look on his face. "Jackson, what in the hell does she think she is doing? Buying me into her damn company?" Jackson didn't answer, as he was already diving into the massive feast set out before them.

After dinner and a drink, the band livened up the crowd. There were several familiar faces among the crowd, mostly authors that Sterling knew. It was a bit loud for him so he decided to take a walk. He strolled out of the other side of the ballroom and into another hallway. He shut the doors behind him to shut out the noise. Ahead of him was a cozy living room with soft shaggy white carpet. Though he had shoes on, he could tell it was one of those carpets just made to make love on. He walked a little further and saw something very familiar on the coffee table. A copy of *Summer Rain*, his last book from Advent Publishers. He picked it up and smiled. She was a fan. This was one of his more erotic novels; he was surprised to see it out in the open like this.

He chuckled to himself and opened the first couple of pages until he reached a blank one. He pulled a pen out of his inside pocket and quickly signed the book personally to Alexandra Tate. He set the book back down and continued his look around. He walked down another hallway and found stairs. Dare he snoop around in her house? The curiosity was killing him. He had to know what her bedroom looked like. With one hand on the railing, he looked back quick to see if anyone was watching or following. With no one around and no sound except the big band coming from the ballroom, he ascended the stairs. They were marble, as was the banister. He was impressed. He reached the top and saw a long hallway with a number of doors. Each door was slightly ajar. There were two bathrooms on the floor, set in between the rooms. The door to the last room in the corridor was closed. *Bingo, he thought. Her bedroom.* He walked slowly down the hall and reached for the brass doorknob. He slowly opened the door, being ever so careful not to make a peep and slipped inside. Once the door closed behind him, he sighed heavily. He made it. He knew Alex would never leave her own party and come searching for him so his nervousness subsided and he looked around. He gasped. Her bedroom was damn near as big as the living room downstairs. There was a huge king sized canopy bed with sheer material flowing all around it. The windows were covered in the same material. The color was odd; it was not white but not pink, more like a champagne color. He walked up to her vanity and touched the edge, getting a feel for Alexandra Tate. There were at least a dozen designer perfumes set out on top of a sparkling circular mirror. Lotions and body sprays covered the vanity. He peeked into the bathroom and laughed. Her whirlpool tub was enormous. There was a copy of another book of his on the edge of the tub. *She really was a fan.*

"Christ, that bath is big enough for two!" he proclaimed out load.

A voice from behind made him jump. "Willing to give it a go, then?" Alex stood at the entryway to her bedroom with her arms crossed and a Cheshire cat grin on her face.

"Shit, Alex, I am sorry. I got lost and just wandered up here. I came in here and it just mesmerized me. You have impeccable taste." Sterling said, hoping his compliments would save his ass, and they did.

"Thank you, Sterling. As I said," Alex spoke softly as she walked directly up to Sterling and fondled his tie. "Want to give it a go?" Her gaze was hypnotizing.

"I...I...I beg your pardon?" Sterling felt his stomach do a somersault and his knees go weak.

"Come on, Sterling, you didn't really think I was the frigid little ice bitch everyone thinks I am did you?"

"N…No, ma'am. Um, I mean Alex. It's just that you caught me off guard that's all."

"I see. Well, relax if you need to then." In one second she had Sterling's tie off and on the floor next to her. She was unbuttoning his shirt when he grabbed her hands.

"Alex, please. Don't" He closed his eyes. "We can't do this. It is unprofessional."

He could not concentrate with her around him. In the next second, a pair of soft, warm lips were pressed up against his. He wanted to open his eyes so badly but he didn't. He tried pulling away but she wouldn't let him so he stopped running and gave in. He kissed her back, long and hard. His hands went to the small of her back and then one dropped to her firm bottom. She moaned ever so slightly and Sterling lost all composure. His passion met hers and vice versa. They stood there kissing passionately for the longest time, their tongues engulfing each other, moans and whispers escaping. Alex felt the hardness pressing up against her and saw her chance. She was finally going to have him once and for all. She was going to see if he was the same man that he wrote about. Sterling lifted Alex off her feet and carried her over to the bed, not once parting from her lips. Her dainty hands were wrapped around his neck. He gently laid her down, carefully unzipping her dress as he went. He was not really surprised to see she had nothing on underneath. Alex did all she could to not stare at the bulge in his pants. It was massive! Her eyes gleamed. Sterling quickly removed her garment from the bed and hung it up for her and returned to his duties. He had removed his tuxedo jacket and shoes and unzipped his pants. Alex's fingers and long nails wrapped around Sterling's manhood. He gasped and closed his eyes. She could not do this yet. He pushed her away and removed the rest of his clothing. He then walked to the end of the bed and started crawling up her way. He had a devious smile on his face; Alex loved every minute of it. He grabbed hold of her thighs and pushed them apart as far as he could. She was tall, so her long legs went pretty far, which left Sterling plenty of room for tasting her delicacies. He knelt between her legs and bent down and went to work.

Alex lifted right off the bed. Sterling had to hold her down the whole time he was eating her, as she was ready to explode every time he dove in further. He finally stopped, after letting her come three times. She lay there, breathless. He climbed on top of her and entered her slowly. She gasped at the size of him inside her. She just could not believe it.

Why was this man not a porn star? He started slowly at first and then gave up and just started rocking and pumping as fast as he could. It felt so good to be inside her. He bent his long neck down and grabbed an erect nipple in his mouth and gave it a quick bite. Alex came again. And then a fifth time. She just could not believe it! And he was not finished yet. He rolled her over and pulled up on her hips so that he was entering her from behind. He reached around and rolled her already swollen clit between his fingers as he slid into her from behind. She came again. He grabbed her hips and thrust in her as hard as he could and she let out a wail. He knew he was hurting her but he knew she loved every minute of it as well. He pounded on her until he could not take it any longer. They both exploded together in a fury of fireworks and stars. The impulses going through their bodies had the power of a locomotive. Alex dropped down and Sterling dropped down right on top of her, kissed her again and rolled off of her. Neither one of them said a word for quite some time, both of them trying to regulate their breathing.

Alex was the first to speak. "Sterling. Where have you been? I see why you write so passionately in your books. Oh my God. That was earth shattering."

"Well, thank you, Alex. I cannot say I did all the work though. You are quite amazing yourself." Sterling really did not know what to think of all this now. Alex suddenly got up and went into the bathroom and closed the door. When she came out half an hour later, she looked just like she did an hour ago when she walked into her room, minus the gown. She smiled and reached for the gown and slipped it on.

"I have a bedroom for you here on this floor. You are more than welcome to stay." She smiled deviously and left Sterling alone. He quickly got up and washed up, used some men's cologne he had found and got dressed to go join the party. *What was happening to him?*

Sterling woke up in Alexandra Tate's bedroom. He quickly sat up, not remembering at all how he ended up there. He remembered the events earlier in the evening in her bedroom, but after that, things got a bit fuzzy. He knew he talked to Jack about leaving the party early and Jack would not let him. He sat up, glad to see Alex was not there. There was a tray next to the bed full of breakfast for him. He shrugged his shoulders and dove in. After a hot shower, Sterling got dressed quickly and set out to find Miss Tate. He ran into Celia and Jack coming out of their bedroom. They both grinned at him.

"How was your evening, Mr. Morris?" Celia asked, knowing all along about Alexandra's fantasies about him. Sterling blushed and walked past them.

"Fine, thank you, Celia. Have either of you seen Miss Tate?" Jackson and Celia followed him downstairs and into the kitchen for some hot coffee after responding to him with giggles. Everything from the night before had been cleaned up impeccably. It looked as if nothing had happened the night before.

"Our flight leaves in three hours, Sterling. Have you decided if you are going to sign with Tate or not?" Jackson sipped on his coffee hoping his friend had come to his senses and would sign with the company. He would be set for life.

"We didn't even talk about it, did we? Hell, I don't know. I feel so bad about Cliff. I feel like I am betraying him."

"Sterling, Cliff said himself that he wanted you to sign. The past is past, leave it that way. And from the looks of things, you and Miss Tate have quite a future anyhow." Jackson grinned at Sterling. Sterling ignored the comment, still wondering why he could not remember anything from the night before.

"Where is she anyhow? I don't remember going to bed at all last night." Sterling left the kitchen to walk in search of Alexandra Tate and some answers. He found her curled up in her living room in a silk robe and matching slippers, in her big chair with one of his books. He smiled, remembering that she was a fan. He walked in quietly.

"I am glad to see that my body is not all you are a fan of." Sterling blushed at his forwardness. Alex looked up, startled to see him standing there and put her book down to join him.

"I didn't hear you come in, Sterling. Come in, sit down. Thank you so much for signing the book, it means a lot to me." She blushed, which was rare for her, but Sterling signed it knowing that it would get to her. He wrote: *To Alexandra—I hear you are quite a fan. All my love, Sterling.* She did not want to know how he knew, but she knew he did.

"Don't mention it, Alex. Always willing to please a fan."

"And that you do, Mr. Morris. You most certainly do." Sterling blushed again as Alex reached over and kissed him full on the lips, her tongue exploring his mouth, her breath fresh and hot. Sterling pulled away, holding her on the shoulders.

"Alex, we can't here. Jackson and Celia are down the hall in the kitchen."

"Yes, I know. And they both drink about five cups of coffee each in the morning with their newspapers." Alex pushed him back against the couch and untied her robe. It fell open revealing her perfect body. Sterling felt himself stiffen at once. *Dammit, she was gorgeous.* Her black silken hair fell over her shoulders, her black silky patch all curly and glistening, waiting for his touch. He reached out, stroking her lightly. She gasped and threw her head back, arching her back to meet his fingers. Her breasts hung perfectly in front of him. Alex reached down and unzipped his Levis that he rarely wore and unleashed his rock hard muscle. She kneeled in front of him and put the whole length of him into her mouth, which was so warm and inviting. He moaned and remembered they had other guests in the house. He forgot to care. She sucked harder and faster, making Sterling's hands grasp at anything he could find. One hand found her head and the other found the side of the couch. His eyes rolled in the back of his head as her tongue lassoed his hard cock, doing tricks to it that even he had never written about. He exploded in her mouth, letting her swallow every drop of his love juice. He sighed. "All right, all right, I will sign with you, Alexandra."

SEVEN

The next two weeks were pure chaos at Tate Publishing, with all submissions coming to a halt to welcome the new starring author, Sterling Morris. Alexandra had also managed to pick up seven more well-known authors at her party and got them to sign, though her methods of persuasions were quite different from that of Sterling's. Sterling had decided against Alexandra's wishes, and wished to remain in Milwaukee. This is where he was from and this is where he liked to write. He liked his little office. Besides, he liked being close to Jack, since he was his editor and did not expect them to move for him. Alexandra had thrown a little tantrum but soon got over it. She set Sterling up with her marketing director right away to get him started on advertising for his new book, press releases and book signings. Sterling hated to admit it, but all the attention was exciting as hell. He had just finished his next book *Cabana Nights* and had his nose buried every night in his new book, which had Alex Tate as his main character. Not realistically of course, but Sterling loved to pretend it was really her he was writing about. Jackson and Celia had taken Sterling out to dinner to celebrate. Sterling called Clifford Ardent to give him the news. He was glad to hear Sterling finally came to his senses but was not the most cheerful person to talk to. Justin had just returned home from another round of chemotherapy was just taking its toll on the poor kid. Sterling told Cliff to give Justin his love and made a mental note to send the kid something.

Alex was thriving in her office. She loved the way people smiled and envied her when she did something magnificent. She was delighted to finally have Sterling in her company, though very disappointed he would not move. She decided to give him a month or so and try again. Sterling got to see the other side of Alexandra Tate when Arnold, the former Head of Submissions, returned from vacation only to find out that he had been demoted and was humiliated in front of the whole company, Alexandra's specialty. Alex marched right out of her office when she heard he was there.

"Arnold! Get your ass over here right now!" As the whole office went dead silent, Arnold walked up to her with his head bowed.

"Yes, Miss Tate?"

"What in the fuck were you thinking by leaving on vacation with a shitload of submissions sitting on your desk with a deadline for the end of the day?" Alex was tapping her high heeled toe on the floor with her arms crossed in front of her and stormy clouds rolling in her eyes.

"I am sorry, Miss Tate but my flight…" Alex quickly interrupted him.

"I don't give a shit if you had to cancel your whole damn vacation! You know the deadline. You could have delegated your work before you left. No thanks to you, Madison and I took them all home and got them finished in record time. Oh yes, and you can switch desks with Amee. She is now Head of Submissions. Maybe next time, before you decide to go off on your time, you will get the job done that I pay you to do."

"Yes, Miss Tate." Arnold quickly ran back to his office to clear it out and switch desks with Amee, silently cursing Alex Tate under his breathe.

Sterling stood at the edge of her doorway with his jaw dropped and his eyes bulging out. He could not believe what a bitch she really was. The rumors really were true. He chuckled to himself but then realized that he really did not want to be a part of this company with that kind of management. He decided to stick it out and see what they did with his book. Alex sat in her chair and motioned for him to come in and sit down.

"Sorry you had to see that, Sterling, but some people just need to realize their place around here." Alex said without even looking up.

"Don't you think you were a bit hard on him, Alex? I mean, Christ, right in front of everyone?" Sterling could still not believe the change in personality from when he had first met her. Alex shrugged it off.

"Really, Sterling, who's side are you on? He could have cost us valuable time by not meeting the deadlines and time is books, books are money! Enough of that anyhow, it is old news already. How is everyone here treating you? Did Vicki get you all set up in marketing?"

Sterling decided to let is pass and changed subjects with her. "Yes, thank you. She is quite remarkable in the ways of public relations, really. I was quite impressed."

"Great. If you think she is remarkable, wait until you see what she has done with your book cover."

"My book cover?! They didn't change it, did they?" Sterling damn near had a heart attack. He and his cover artist had worked together for weeks on that!

"Settle down, settle down." Alex put her hand up for him to calm down and pressed a button on her phone. "Madison, will you send Antonio in here now, please?"

"Right away, Miss Tate" came the southern response. A few minutes later, Antonio, head of the Art Department, walked in carrying several posters and fliers and forms.

"Sterling, this is what Vicki had done with your cover." Alex said sweetly as Antonio laid them all out in front of Sterling. Sterling could not believe his eyes. There were giant posters of his book covers with his name on them. There were bookmarks, postcards, and 8×10 glossies, all of his book cover, which looked absolutely spellbinding. The man and woman on the cover on the beach were nude, and though you could not see any private parts; it left little to the imagination. Sterling smiled and was speechless. He just could not imagine this much publicity.

"I don't know what to say, Alex. Thank

you so much."

"Don't mention it, darling. It will all pay off when we get you started on your book tour. Speaking of, you need to stop by Elizabeth's desk. She is over in Vicki's department. She will be the one setting up your schedule for the book tour. All you need to do is show up at the airports where you are scheduled to be and everything else will be taken care of. Elizabeth or Vicki will be escorting you on all your tours, getting the book signings set up and cleaning up afterwards. You just be there. Any questions?"

"Yes, where the hell were you ten years ago, Alex?"

"Just blooming, Mr. Morris, just blooming. Just ask Clifford about that. He remembers the old days. Now, if you will excuse me, I have tons of work to do and you have a full day ahead of you before you get back to Milwaukee." Alex dismissed him as quickly as she found him. He understood, she was a busy woman. He strolled out of her office, his head held high, in search of Elizabeth.

Sterling found Elizabeth Houghton sitting at her desk, phone to her ear, busy chatting with some new bookstore in the area. She glanced up and saw Sterling, smiled and motioned for him to come in and sit down. Sterling was in awe. Elizabeth was a blonde bombshell. She had strawberry blonde hair down to the middle of her back, big beautiful brown eyes and smile that would break any man's heart. He sat in the chair in front of her. She was a nice change from Alexandra, he could tell by the way she talked on the phone. She was pleasant and polite and never demanding. Not that Alex wasn't a hottie, but not a natural beauty, inside and out. Elizabeth ended her call and stood up with her hand extended.

"It is a pleasure to meet you, Mr. Morris. I am so glad we will be working together on your book tour."

"Please, Sterling will be fine. Can I call you Elizabeth?" Sterling smiled his gentleman smile, his smile that was dashing and melted the hearts of the few women he entertained.

"Oh, of course you can. Everyone else does. So, what do you think about all of this? Are you overwhelmed yet?"

"Not really overwhelmed yet, but it is all very exciting. I feel like a damned celebrity around here! I am just an author like everyone else. I don't understand all the fuss."

"Well, surely you know how hard Miss Tate was trying to get you in here." Elizabeth rolled her eyes at the thought.

"Ah, yes. Miss Tate. She is quite a character, isn't she?"

"She can be. She never gives me a hard time or anyone in this department actually, because we are the ones who make her money. Besides, my father was great friends with Edward Tate before he died, so I think she feels obligated to me for some reason. Nonetheless, I don't care, it's job security." She laughed a sweet laugh, a sexy laugh. Sterling was surrounded by stunning women and people who thought he was God. How much better could it get?

"Here is a tentative schedule of the first half of your tour. It will last for three months and go to 12 different states, a week in each one. You will have two days off during the week, but not on the weekends, as that is when the book signings are huge. I will get everything set up for you on each one, you just show up at the airports and hotels listed and we will take care of you. Actually, I will be tagging along at the same airports and hotels so it is not like we are leaving you alone anywhere. The books will all be shipped out as soon as they roll off the press, which I have been told is next week. They will have the galley for you to review tomorrow. The cover art is already done, as you have seen. Any questions?"

Sterling sat there taking it all in. A three-month book tour? Do they know how many books he can sell in that time?

"What about my writing, Elizabeth? I can't not write anything for three months?"

"Covered. You will be getting a laptop to take with you for in the hotel or wherever you need to write! No way we are going to smother your talent!!" He thanked Elizabeth, shook her hand and left Tate Publishing for the day. He had to get back to Alex's place and cool down, this was becoming overwhelming. Alex had insisted he stay at her place and not in a hotel in downtown Jackson. He took a cab over to her place and let himself in. He walked straight to the bar and poured himself a Southern Comfort on the rocks. He needed to relax and unwind; it was going to be a long journey.

EIGHT

Jackson and Celia had a little surprise party waiting for Sterling when he returned to Milwaukee four days later than planned. He really was just not in the mood for it. Alex and him had just had their first official fight. How in the hell did he get into a relationship with this woman? He went to her party, does not remember half of it, was seduced by her, slept with her, a few times, and signed with her. The next thing he knew, he was her boyfriend. That was going to stop. He had tried telling her this was business and sleeping with her was an added bonus. She never blew up and turned into the cold-hearted woman he saw at her office, but she was obviously very disappointed. She had every number to all of the hotels he was going to stay at during his book tour and planned on checking up on him. That is when he put his foot down. She was not his keeper. Celia laughed it off, telling him to watch it, as Alex always gets what she wants. Jackson told him to ignore her and keep looking elsewhere, there were going to be lots of women after him. After a short night of drinking with his friends, Sterling had to excuse himself to go home. Jet lag had set in and he had to get himself primed for the tour that was starting soon. As soon as he walked in the door, his phone rang. He knew it was Alex. He thought of her and how sexy she really was. He just could not resist her; she was so damn beautiful.

"Hello, Alex." He said without even waiting to see if it was her or not.

"How did you know it was me, Sterling?" Alex asked in a childlike voice.

"You have me pinned, Alex. I swear you have me on satellite. What can I do for you my dear?" he asked, trying to make it short and sweet so he could get some sleep.

"You can do a lot for me, Sterling, honey, if you were here. Starting with that ever so talented tongue of yours. Oh how I do love that, baby, when you use it all over me." Sterling closed his eyes, thinking of the last time they made love. He had licked her from head to toe, driving her out of her mind. He had given her nine orgasms, a personal record for her, and for him as well. He smiled, cherishing the moment, feeling himself grow hard beneath his khakis.

"Alex, you know you drive me crazy when you talk like that sweetheart. Now let's save it for when we are together or I swear, girl, you are going to be taking the midnight flight to Milwaukee." He reached down and unzipped his pants and pulled out his rock hard muscle. He could hear Alex's breathing getting heavy and he knew what she was doing.

"But Sterling, darling, I am going to miss you so much when you are gone. I don't think I can live without you or your tongue for that long. You just make me so...so damn hot, Sterling." She moaned as her fingers intertwined with her soft silky hair down below and pressed against her, pressing her oh so sensitive spots.

"Alex, please. Oh my God, woman, you just don't realize what you do to me. I wish you were here right now so I could look at your beautiful naked body. So I can rub you and lick you all over. So I can do things that would just make you shiver. I want you Alexandra."

"Sterling, I want you too. Let me come up there. I know you are busy packing, but please, just let me. One more goodbye before you leave on your tour. Sterling, I am so wet for you right now."

"Alex, I can't. Not tonight...."

"You are standing there with your cock in your hands, I know you are.
Don't tell me you can't tonight. You know

you want it as bad as I do...."

Sterling dreamed of their phone call, and of his jacking himself off in the middle of his living room and Alexandra masturbating on the other end. It was a nice release before going to bed. That was at 10 PM and it was now 4 AM. Sterling felt a soft, delicate hand running down the side of his body. He always slept nude at his house since he was the only one there. Well, usually.

He opened his eyes and rubbed the sleep from them. They focused on Alex Tate, kneeling over him with nothing on. He looked again. Yep, it was her.

"How in the hell..." he started to ask. She put a manicured fingernail over his lips and shushed him. She smiled her devious smile and went to work on him, instantly waking up all parts of him. They made love to each other until 8 am that morning; both exhausted but very satisfied and fell into a deep sleep.

The next morning, Alex explained to Sterling that it was nice to have friends in high places. One of her bookstore execs that lived near her had his own private jet and flew her up here. He was to meet her back at the airport today in about an hour. Alex was busy getting ready to go.

"How do you do it, Alex?" Sterling asked, watching her every move.

"Do what, Mr. Morris?" She always called him that when she was joking around.

"Live every day with this much commitment? Hahah. You fly up here, fuck my brains out, and fly right home, like it is nothing for you to do this every day."

"Now don't start giving me ideas. I just wanted to give you a little goodbye kiss." She smiled, kissed him passionately and walked towards the door.

"Hell, if this morning was a kiss...I wonder what making love really is."

"Goodbye Sterling. Good luck on your tour, I know you will do just great. Elizabeth will take great care of you." And then she was gone again. Just like that. Sterling jumped up. *Elizabeth! She was meeting him at the airport. He smiled and got packing. She was a beauty he was going to seduce all on his own.* Sterling showered and changed and got everything packed. He went to his office and grabbed all his discs for his writing while he was on the road. He was so damn excited he almost forgot to call Elizabeth to confirm everything. They were to leave in three days. His books were hot off the press as they were speaking.

Elizabeth had one of them in her hands. He laughed as he thought how steamed Alex would be because she missed the first books coming off the press. Oh well, time well spent. Sterling was so excited that his book was finally out and was dying to see it. Elizabeth overnighted him five copies for himself. He could expect them in tomorrow's mail. He realized he had already packed and they were not leaving for three days. He felt embarrassed from the anxiousness he was feeling at getting started. He was not usually this childlike when it came to events like this. That woman was doing it to him. Alex Tate, the evil seductress. He laughed to himself again. Elizabeth was rattling on about the first book signing in Chicago. It was at Barnes & Noble, so it was sure to be a big hit. Elizabeth and Sterling talked for an hour about their lives, learning more about each other. They never realized it until one of them got another call and looked at the time.

"Elizabeth, I am sorry I took up your time, I will see you in a few days then in the windy city."

"Not to worry, Sterling. Time with you is well spent. I will see you in Chicago." They hung up and Sterling stood there. *Was she coming on to him?*

Alex landed in Nashville just in time to quick stop by her house, shower and change and run to work. Sterling's book came out today and she wanted to be one of the first ones to see it. The press releases were out, there were already orders coming in and advance orders to fill. As Alex walked into the office, she noticed there was an unusual amount of buzzing around the office, everyone was talking about something. Then she saw it. She stopped in her tracks and everyone stopped in midsentence. Sterling's book was all over the office. Everyone had seen it already. She wanted to be the first one to see it. She looked around at everyone who was waiting on pins and needles for her to explode but she didn't this time. She pursed her lips together and walked quickly into her office and slammed the door so hard the glass shook. There was a stack of the books on her desk as requested. If she would have been in the office at 6 am like she usually was, this would not have happened, so she could not blame her employees. She sat down in her chair and looked at one of the books. Her guys in the art department were just awesome. This book was going to be hard to keep on the shelves. She felt a best seller in her hands. She picked up the phone and dialed Sterling's number. She barely let him answer when she told him about his book.

"Yes, I know Alex. Elizabeth was going to overnight them but she sent them over same day FedEx. They look awesome—you guys really did an awesome job. I don't know how to thank y…" There was a loud click on the other end. "Alex? Hello?" That was odd he thought. Maybe she just got caught up in something or had to go. He let it go and kept on admiring his books.

That bitch! Elizabeth had sent Sterling his books ASAP and Alex wanted to be the one to share his excitement. She couldn't even yell at Elizabeth, she was out of the office now for three months working with Sterling on his book tour. *What a day this is turning out to be…*

NINE

Angelina Frost leaned forward with a scowl, covering her more than her pretty face, her eyes projecting an icy stare. Punching the illustrations lying on the surface of her desk with one long perfect manicured fingernail, she allowed her gaze to go up to the thin, speckled man dressed in a crimson pullover sweater, jeans and designer athletic shoes, who was fighting hard to maintain his composure under her unrelenting scrutiny.

She threw herself back in her high-backed Italian leather chair, hitting the armrests with her open palms, causing the man in front of her desk to jump despite his anticipation.

"Earl, this is not what I asked you to create." Before he could answer, she smiled something, bordering on pure evil. "Yes, you're right. If I had the artistic talent, I could have done these portfolios myself. Unfortunately I don't. I was only given the talent to take this advertising company to the very top of the industry."

As Angelina pointed at the man, her eyes narrowed. "For those things I need and cannot create on my own, I hire people with the talent to create what I can imagine, and that means you. If you are unwilling or unable to imagine and produce what I have asked you to do, by God, I'll search until I do. Even if that means firing the whole Goddamn art department. Am I understood?"

Earl crossed his waist with one arm, held the other out with his hand broken at the wrist, assuming a feminine pose. "Of course, I understand. I also thought those designs were exactly what you described in our department meeting."

Her voice was hostile and cold. Her expression frozen. "Well, you were wrong. Dead wrong." Angelina made a sweeping gesture with her hand.
"This isn't even close to what I wanted." With the realization her threat was real; Earl put on hand on his chin and rocked back on the balls of his feet. "Perhaps if you went over what you want one more time, I will be better able to convey to my staff precisely what it is that you want."

Angelina leaned on her desk with her elbows, chin cradled in her hands. Her expression had changed to something totally innocent and angelic, disguising the malevolence, hiding just underneath the surface. "No, Earl, not one more time. The last fucking time. If you and your staff can't get the covers right this time, I'll search until I find me a staff who fucking can and will!"

His voice was breaking. He gestured at her desk. "If you will, please explain what you want depicted in the portfolio."

Angelina picked up the one closest to her and held it up between her two hands. "This one depicts the strength I want, but there is no softness of a woman." She picked up the next one. "This one has the ferocity, but not the gentleness to appeal to a woman."

Earl held one finger out in front of himself. "Let me see if my thinking is correct."

Angelina smiled a veiled warning. "Be my guest."

"In the cover for the women's athletic shoes, we might have a competitive, challenging and grueling sport but then the beauty and femininity of a woman."

"See how easy it is when you take a meaningful scene from your head and put it into the design."

Earl put his hand in front of his mouth to hide the overwhelming relief he felt. "I used that analogy because it was my favorite ad."

Angelina stood up with her hands on her hips. "If you'll find a design in each of these ads like you're talking about here, you'll hit a home run with each of them."

"In that case," Earl said with happiness and gratitude ringing in his voice, "why don't I get the hell out of here and get back to what I do best." Angelina pointed toward the door with an absolutely neutral expression.

"There's the door."

Hesitating before he went out, he turned back with a smile. "When we have something for you to see, I'll let you know. We'll get this done is we have to work all night."

"I'll be waiting," she said, daring to let a smile on her lips, quickly turning into a warning. "Make sure you don't take beyond 3:00 pm tomorrow. That's the last possible time we can get to the printers and ship them on time." When Earl threw up his hand and started to leave, Angelina said, "And Earl?"

He stopped in mid-stride and looked back uncertainly. "Yes?"

"Don't forget to close the door."

Earl smiled weakly before closing the

door and running down the hall before she could change her mind and call him back for more of the same.

Angelina sat down and turned her back to the door. She smiled, thinking all she had to do was kick the right ass and scare some sense to someone's head to get the job done right. Satisfied her duties as president of a corporate empire had been successfully carried out and the workday was drawing to a close, she allowed her mind to wonder.

She was invited and expected to attend a very high profile soirée for executives in the various positions in the advertising industry later in the evening. When the invitation first arrived, she had just returned from shopping and had bought several new outfits - one of which she planned to
wear. The dress was very low cut with tiny little straps that would showcase her generous assets beautifully.

Ken Norton, the avowed bi-sexual, had a special fondness for breasts, playing with and sucking them until they were sore to the touch the next day, or so she had been told. She had never personally had the chance to get very close to him before, but tonight things would be different. She vowed to make a point to find out just how fond he was of a pair of perfect thirty-sixes with pointy nipples, and in the process, see for herself whether the rumor was true that Ken was hung like a Greek god's horse.

Once they had made a connection, she would hurry him back to her penthouse. With the home turf advantage, she would make sure he was comfortable. Following some deep kissing and heavy mutual physical exploration, making sure she kept his hands just shy of his intended prize before she excused herself to the bedroom. Safely behind closed doors, she would change into nothing but a pale white, almost transparent silk gown, leaving nothing to his imagination.

She could call to him through the door, inviting him to join her. When he came through the door, she would have her first clue about the true size of his love muscle, pushing out the front of his pants. Regardless, she would go to him and force his hands to his side, taking charge from that point on. Based on her past experience, she wondered whether a bisexual would be as thrilled as the other men who had been subject to her own personal brand of lovemaking.

Regardless, once they were naked and in the middle of her perfectly round bed with red satin sheets, she would disable his hands each time he tried to be an active participant. She would put him on his back and start with his perfectly shaped lips, working her way down to his toes, kissing and fondling every square inch of the front of his body without taking him in her mouth.

Turning him over on his stomach, she would repeat the process. Except this time, she would linger on the cheeks of his ass before rimming his asshole with her tongue until he screamed out in ecstasy. By the time she rolled him over again, he would have hold of his throbbing, monstrous hard manhood, desperately trying to slip him in her honey walls. On this night, their first night together, that would not be a part of her agenda. Her hands, mouth and throat would be the main attraction. Even then, he would be given the opportunity to orgasm in her oral cavity time and again until he had to call it quits.

Whether or not Ken would ever be allowed to explore her hairy delights with anything but his tongue and fingers would indeed depend on the size of his organ.

Should Ken prove to be to absolutely huge, even extensive lubrication could not stand off the damage that could only be corrected by a skilled surgeon. So if Ken proved to be as big as some of her female acquaintances reputed him to be, theirs was destined to be an oral romance.

"Excuse me, ma'am," a voice called from her door, bringing her out of a very pleasant introspection.

When Angelina turned her chair around, she found her secretary, leaning in the doorway. "Yes, Judy?'

"It's five o'clock, ma'am. I just wondered whether you wanted me for anything else before I left for the day."

"No, you go ahead," Angelina answered, slightly embarrassed to have been caught at such a personal moment but forced a pleasant smile. "You've done more than you're share for one day."

"In that case," Judy said, returning the smile, "I'll be going now, but don't forget the party tonight."

Angelina quickly opened her organizer and pretended to check before she looked up again. "Thanks, Judy. I had completely forgotten about tonight."

"Don't give it another thought. That's

why I'm here." Judy smiled again waved and was gone.

While Angelina was straightening her desk and preparing to leave, she decided to take a long, hot bubble bath, using a special bubble soap she had recently purchased before dressing for the get-together. If everything went right tonight, she wanted Ken to remember the smell of wild flowers while he lingered between her legs rather than a foul smell from cannery row.

Alexandra shut off Sterling's laptop. She felt guilty for opening and digging around but she wanted to peek at his next project. She was impressed, as usual. It wasn't one of the juicier parts of the story, but she liked it. There was just something about that Angelina character she liked. Sterling was in Memphis this week, starting out the book tour in the south. He had done one already in Nashville and had sold over 100 copies of his book. They had to have more delivered down to the store. He was officially now the first author to sell that many books in one book signing in all of Tate Publishing.

Alexandra had called Sterling the night before, but he and Elizabeth were out to dinner. A twinge of jealousy had shot through Alex but she dismissed it as business. They had been together on the book signings for two weeks now and Alex had not heard boo from either of them. The sales and the publicity were rolling in. Sterling was on the news, in the papers. He is the hottest author since Stephen King. She loved the fact that Sterling was getting all the attention and publicity he deserved but hated being second best. She hated the fact that she was not out there sharing it with him. She looked at her watch and quickly jumped up and grabbed her house keys and her purse. It was 7:30 already. She had never been this late for work. She jumped into her limo and told the driver to step on it.

Sterling spent an hour literally signing his signature. It was getting to the point that his wrist was so sore he could barely read his own name. He could not believe his instant stardom. He sold loads of books in Nashville and Memphis proved to be just as prosperous. Elizabeth was great. She introduced him to all the big wigs in the bookstores, guided him around the towns and made sure everything ran smoothly. Plus, she was drop dead gorgeous and sweet as apple pie. *Man, what I wouldn't do for a slice of that*, he thought, as he watched her talking to some customers standing in line. He had avoided Alex purposely the last few days. He was enjoying his time with Elizabeth and he did not want Alex to interfere. He smiled at Elizabeth as she waved and winked at him. Dammit, he just had to have her.

When the book signing was done, they had sold 95 books, another record for the second week on the job. He was just overwhelmed by how fast this was all happening. On top of signing his books, people were asking for his autograph on other things as well, including one woman's breasts. He was an erotica novelist and his reputation preceded him. He laughed when she exposed them right there in the bookstore for the world to see, but they were very nice breasts at that. He signed them as Elizabeth rolled her eyes and laughed. When everything was packed up, and the handshakes were finished, Elizabeth and Sterling headed back towards the rented limousine that took them everywhere. Tate spared no expenses for its starring authors.

"Elizabeth, since we have a day off tomorrow, why don't you join me in my room for breakfast in the morning? I will order for us if you don't mind." Sterling asked her, nervous as hell.

"That would be great. I will be over at about seven if that isn't too early for you?" Elizabeth smiled. Her pearly white teeth shined through her red lips beautifully. Sterling felt himself growing hard and tried to change the subject.

"Great, so what did you think about today? I mean, is this all for real? It is all happening so fast!" They talked of the day's event and went back to their respective hotel rooms to recuperate from a long day.

Sterling got out the breakfast menu right away and started ordering everything off the menu. He started with a cold bottle of Cristal Champagne. It was $400.00 a bottle, but everything was on the company and Alex told him to have fun. Had she known he was going to treat another woman with it, she would have said otherwise. He ordered fresh croissants, butter on the side, a dish of cinnamon and sugar, peaches, seedless grapes, strawberries and whipped cream. He had that brought up right away in the morning along with the real breakfast food, the eggs, toast, bacon, french toast, orange juice and coffee. He knew Elizabeth did not eat a lot so he did not overindulge on the food.

Elizabeth showed up promptly at seven o'clock dressed in bright white denim shorts and a white tank top. Her blonde hair was tied up in a ponytail. She looked as fresh as the first Spring rain. He told her so as well, making her blush for the first time. She was shy when it came to compliments. He sat her down and they ate breakfast heartily, talking of the headlines in the newspaper and anything else that sprung to mind. They never spoke of work that morning. Sterling had other things on his mind. He had room service clean up their breakfast dishes, leaving the fruit and croissants on another table. Elizabeth stood up, stretched her arms out, closing her eyes. When she opened them, Sterling was standing nose to nose with her. He ran his hands down her arms, down her sides. She looked deep into his eyes and saw passion in them.

"Sterling, I don't know whether we should be doing this. I..." Elizabeth was stopped with Sterling's mouth over hers. The floor dropped out from under her. The passion in that one kiss just made her completely uninhibited. She matched his passion, returning the kiss just as forcefully, engulfing his mouth with hers, sweeping the inside of his mouth with her tongue, and tasting every bit of him. He stopped to catch his breath and smiled at her. He took the bottom hem on her little tank top and lifted it gently over her head, dropping the shirt on the floor. He reached around and unclipped her bra with one hand, letting that also drop to the floor. She stared at him, not quite sure what he was going to do next. He grabbed the butter, already softened and rubbed it gently over a croissant he had in the other hand and then over her already erect nipple. She gasped at the coolness of the butter and giggled. Sterling then took the cinnamon and sugar and sprinkled it on her nipples over the butter and then over the croissant.

He smiled at her as he leaned down and covered one breast with his mouth, licking and sucking his breakfast off of her. She grabbed his head and held him tight to her chest. Her moans sent him over the edge and he attacked the other one. When they were clean of any cinnamon and butter, he rid her of the rest of her clothes and laid her gently on the bed. He went over to the table and came back with the rest of the champagne they had left from breakfast and poured her another glass. Then he brought over grapes and peaches. The grapes were ice cold, fresh out of the refrigerator. He placed them strategically all over her body. He started with her toes, placing them in between each one, one on her ankle, one in her belly button, in between her breasts and under them as well, in her mouth, and of course, one just in the folds of her pink flesh below. He then took a few more and squeezed them gently all over here, letting the cold juices startle her senses.

She gasped, careful not to squish the grape in her mouth. Sterling went to work. He started at her feet, sucking her toes, eating each grape, licking her ankles, nipping at them, eating her grapes, he went around the treasure spot and to her belly button, licking and sucking, and eating her grape. He made his way to her breasts, sucking and licking as he pulled out each grape from underneath them with his teeth. She was moaning now and the grape down below was about to slide out, as her own juices were flowing. Sterling stopped it from coming out with his tongue. He rolled his tongue around the grape, extending it inside her, licking up the juices that were there. He licked all of the grape juice and her juice from inside her and from on her and then went up to her mouth, looking into her eyes and he devoured her with his mouth, crushing the grape, engulfing her. He did a similar routine with the peaches, only instead of placing them on her, he just took a bite and smeared the wetness and juices all over her, even over her hottest parts, cooling her down. He ended his feast with the strawberries and cream, feeding them to her from his mouth, eating them from her breasts and other places. They ended their morning in the shower together, making more of their own juices and cleaning up all of nature's own.

TEN

A month into Sterling's book tour, Alexandra decided she was going to pop in and surprise Sterling and Elizabeth. Surely, they would be delighted to see her on their tour. Sterling had been doing just phenomenal in book sales and had already sold over two hundred and fifty thousand books, which was just off the charts. Alex was beaming with delight with his progress and tried calling him at least two to three times a week but she rarely got through. If they were not doing a meet and greet or a book signing, the two of them were off gallivanting in whatever city they were in. Alex admitted she was a bit jealous of Elizabeth, getting all the time with Sterling but she kept telling herself it would be worth the wait.

Alexandra's plane landed right on time. She had a limo waiting for her out on the runway so she did not have to deal with anyone from the airport. Faces were pressed up against the big glass windows at the airport to try to get a glimpse of what they thought was a huge celebrity. Alex laughed at them all the time. She gave the name of the hotel to the driver and tried to relax in her seat. She was so excited, relaxing was the last thing on her mind. They arrived at the Hilton at around 7 am. Alex did not bother to go to the desk so they could call Sterling and announce her presence; she went straight to the elevator and straight up to the top floor. She checked herself one last time in the mirrored elevator walls, making sure she looked great for Sterling. When the door opened, she was nervous for some reason, which was not like her. She walked to Sterling's room, cleared her throat and knocked on the door. She expected it to fly open and Sterling to run into her arms but no one answered. She knocked again, harder this time, getting irritated that he would not be in this early in the morning. She finally heard footsteps and she sighed. The door opened and she had a huge grin on her face. Unfortunately, Sterling did not. He stood in front of her, dripping wet, with a towel around his waist. His face immediately paled when he saw Alex.

"Um…Alex…what a great surprise. I…uh…can you wait here while I get dressed?" He tried closing the door but Alex pushed her way right through his arms. He tried to stop her but she barged right in.

"Nonsense, Sterling. Looks like I came

at the right time. I was just thinking of how a cool shower might cool me off. After all, I got a little heated up on the way over here thinking of you." Alex walked towards him when suddenly a voice came from behind her. A voice she knew well.

"Sterling, who was that at the door?" Elizabeth asked with a towel over her head and another wrapping her curves tightly. She stopped dead in her tracks when she spotted Alex.

"Oh shit. Alex. H…Hi. Um, I can leave you two alone if you like."
Elizabeth started to leave when Alex completely exploded.

"What in the fuck is going on here?! Do I pay you to sleep with the clients, Elizabeth? Get your shit and go down to the limo! As of now, you are officially off this assignment! And you!" Alex stood there with her hands on her hips staring at Sterling. He was trying to stop Elizabeth, who had run off to the bathroom to get dressed, just sobbing.

"What are you doing here Alex?" Sterling asked her.

"Obviously interrupting something. I should have known something was up a long time ago! You can finish this book tour by yourself. Elizabeth will be coming back with me to work on other projects, if I decide not to fire her ass. Elizabeth, hurry up!" Alex stomped out the door, feeling utterly humiliated. How dare he make such an ass of her! She was mortified, pissed off and upset. She wanted to kill Elizabeth for taking away her catch. Elizabeth came out of the room with two bags and walked down the hall after Alex, leaving Sterling stand in the hallway with a towel around his waist, shaking his head.

Elizabeth sniveled all the way to the airport listening to Alex yell and scream at her. First she fired her. Then she took it back an decided it would be more fun to just torture her than it would be to not have anyone to yell a all. She thought of poor Sterling and having to do all the tours by himself, with no one there to help promote, set up or take down. She thought of their wonderful breakfast in bed that one morning. She stared out the window, thinking again of how scrumptious everything had tasted on each other when Alex interrupted her thoughts.

"Are you listening to me, dammit!! Christ what the hell do I have to do to get some respect around here! You crossed the line little girl! You are fucking our star author, not to mention my boyfriend. Have you lost your fucking mind, Elizabeth? What in the hell has gotten into you? Besides Sterling I mean. Jesus Christ! You have never acted like this before. You know, I think I am going to take you out of marketing. Maybe I will send Robert down to Dallas to be with Sterling so he doesn't fuck anything else up. At least I will be protecting my investments."

The rest of the trip was silent on both parts. Elizabeth was trying to get up the courage to quit her job but she just could not do it. Her life was at Tate. She knew her job and she knew it well. She drifted off to sleep on the airplane, dreading walking into the office with everyone knowing what happened. And she was right.

As soon as Alex walked back into the office with Elizabeth, the whole place went so quiet, you could have heard a pin drop. Everyone froze, waiting for something to happen and it did. Elizabeth started walking in the opposite direction of Alexandra Tate to sit and sulk at her desk for a while when Alex blew up again.

"Yes, that's right, everyone. Get a good

look at what hard working does to you. Elizabeth seems to think here that the best way to promote our clients is to fuck them, right sweetie?! You know what—I don't think I will keep you around to torture you, I think I will fire you. Why don't you get your shit and get the hell out of this office and I don't ever want to see your pretty little face in this building or around Mr. Morris ever again, am I clear?!" Alex yelled so loud the last couple of words out of her mouth cracked from a dry throat. Elizabeth spun on her heel and stomped right back to Alex. Alex's eyes widened, as no one has ever stood up to her before.

"You know what Alex? For just one minute, if you could stop being such a fucking bitch all your life and realize what people's true potentials are, you may get somewhere. I don't mean being top publisher, being rich and famous and having a fucking limo everywhere you go. I am talking about friends, Alex, cause you have none! Nobody here likes you! You treat people like shit, you run them down and you think your shit doesn't stink. Well, let me tell you something baby, you have fucked with the last person in this damn company. You are not firing me because I quit!"

Elizabeth did not even go to her desk and get her things; she walked right out the door. Alex stood there gawking at her. She knew all eyes were on here so she went into her office and slammed the door, not coming out the rest of the day.

Alex sat at her desk for the whole day throwing papers around, wiping tears from her eyes. Her door was locked, not that anyone dared knock on it anyhow, in the mood she was in. How could he stand there and let her look like a complete ass like that? She was just furious. She wanted to throw him out on his ass right along with Elizabeth but she knew the company needed him and that would just cause a scandal. Now she had to face the music and get on with everything in a professional manner like she always did. Her phone had been ringing all day and she never answered it, she let them all go into her voicemail. Finally, at about three that afternoon she could not take it anymore and she grabbed her phone.

"Yes?!" she yelled into the phone. It was Sterling.

"Why, Alex, what a professional way to answer your phone this afternoon. Something eating you?" He sounded calm as hell. Alex was not sure whether to scream at him or hold her cool.

"What is it, Mr. Morris, I have a lot to do today." She tried being as calm as he sounded.

"My my, back on a formal basis are we?"

"Sterling, you chose this path yourself now cut the crap. What do you want?"

"Well, I figured since we both got what we wanted that it is time for a little more negotiation."

"What are you talking about?"

"Well, it is rather obvious that you only wanted me in your company for two reasons, Alex—sex and money. You wanted to fuck the man who wrote the books you get off on every night and make a fortune by getting his books sold. Am I getting warm?" Alexandra's face was bright red and you could damn near see the steam coming from her ears.

"Sterling, that is private information. If you so much as tell…"
Sterling cut her off.

"Oh please, Alex. I could give a shit what you do in your personal time. I want Elizabeth back on my tour or I quit. Right here, right now and I take all of my books with me and I sue your company. I am sure my lawyers can come up with something along the lines of slander, verbal and emotional abuse, who knows what else but I will drag you and your company through the mud." He could hear Alex gasping for air. She was speechless.

"Well, I see you have an agenda. I would love to help you Mr. Morris, but you see Elizabeth quit this morning when she returned so I cannot put her back on your tour. So, if you will just stop all this whining, go back to your book signings and sell some more books like you are supposed to be doing. They won't sell themselves now, will they?" Alex was just about to hang up when Sterling interrupted her little moment of glory she thought she had.

"Well, then you better find her and get her back or I am out of here, Alex. And I won't think twice about it." There was a loud click and Alex sat there with the phone still to her ear. *That son of a bitch. How dare he tell her what to do!* Still, she knew he meant business so she called in Madison to try to reach Elizabeth.

ELEVEN

For two weeks, Sterling had to do his tour by himself. He missed Elizabeth badly. She was all he thought about during the day. He tried calling her but she would not return his calls. He called Alex, who had also left messages with Elizabeth, only to get no response from her either. He thought of Alex and Elizabeth and how different they were—in person and in bed. Alex was wild and vivacious where Elizabeth was soft and sensual. Alex did not care about anyone's feelings or who she stepped on in the path of righteousness in her mind but Elizabeth was just the opposite. He was giving up great sex with Alex, this was true, but it didn't matter. Elizabeth made up for all of it.

He was in Los Angeles, signing away books left and right; so fast his wrist was starting to hurt. He stopped to take a ten-minute break and when he looked up, Elizabeth was walking towards him with a giant smile on her face. He immediately ran over to her and took her up in his arms. She felt so good to hold.

"I am so glad you came back, Elizabeth. I have missed you terribly."

"I am sorry I did not call you, Sterling. I had some things I needed to get worked out. I want to talk to you about something." Sterling grabbed her hand and led her to the table where he was sitting.

"Anything, what is it darling?"

"Actually, it can wait until over dinner, as it requires a lot of attention and detail. Can you have dinner with me tonight?"

"With you or on you?" Sterling asked. Elizabeth blushed as Sterling kissed her on the lips and went back to signing his books, happy as a jaybird now that she was there. Elizabeth thought of Alex and how she wished she could see her face when they broke the news to her.

Angelina Frost locked her office door behind her and turned to stare at the sexy hunk of man that was leaning against her desk. She had not gotten laid in a week and she was long overdue. He looked up when he heard the lock and smiled sheepishly at her. He was all of about twenty-five years old and just starting in the art department. She needed to interview him really thoroughly. She walked slowly over to him, unbuttoning her blazer on the way. His mouth went dry and he tried to back up but he was already against the desk.

"Miss Frost, what are you doing? What if someone needs to see you?"
Anthony asked her nervously.
"Fuck them, Anthony. Fuck them all. They are all pretty useless to me anyhow, I don't really give a shit if they have to wait all damn day." She had her blazer off with nothing on underneath except a push up bra. Anthony felt himself harden in front of her. She noticed immediately and like a magician, she unbuckled his belt and unzipped his pants in about 5 seconds flat. His jeans were falling down as she leaned into him. Her soft breasts felt so good against his warm chest. He grabbed her ass cheeks in his hands and gave a firm squeeze. They were firm all right. He lifted her skirt and was not surprised that there was nothing underneath except for a soaking wet love canal. He picked her up and she wrapped her legs around him. He leaned over with one arm around her and swept off her desk, making everything crash to the floor. He lay her down on her desk and dropped his boxers. She had lust in voice and passion in her eyes. He pulled her to the edge of the desk and thrust himself inside

her. She let out a holler that everyone probably heard. He didn't care; he was quitting after this piece of ass. She was moaning and squealing with every hard thrust he gave her. He held her legs high in the air and just kept on banging. He finally came and decided to leave it in her, she could clean up the mess. She was irritated he did that but in the heat of the moment she really didn't care. He stood back and pulled up his boxers and jeans as she lay there. She came right along with him so she knew she was a mess, but damn was it good. She stood up as he was walking towards the door with a grin on his face.

"That good, was it?" Angelina felt victorious as she straightened herself out and buttoned up her blazer. Anthony opened the door wide and walked out buckling his belt and laughed out loud as people started looking. Angelina's face flushed, as she knew people knew what had just happened. She was about to yell at him when he stopped and turned around.

"Thanks for the great lay, Angelina! Sorry, but I don't think this job is cut out for me!" he yelled loudly as laughed as he walked out the front door. People in the office started laughing right along with him

as Angelina Frost slammed her office door to save herself from further humiliation.

Sterling laughed as he wrote his book about Alexandra Tate, the ice queen of the publishing world. He pulled out of his contract two months after Elizabeth came back to his book tour. They finished up the tour with no more hassles from Alex and then they both quit. Elizabeth started her own public relations company and did all of Sterling's marketing for him. They went back to Discovery Printing, who actually was not doing too badly. They were ecstatic to have Sterling on board and let him do everything his way. Alex, of course, was furious that everything turned out that way and became more bitter than ever before. Her friends even stopped coming to her parties.

There was one party that Alex was not going to miss and that was the release party of *The Heat of the Ice Queen* by Thomas Williams. She had remembered his name because Madison and her had gotten extremely excited over his manuscript and ended up sleeping together. She had never met the author but he declined their contract when she offered it to him, much to her disappointment. This could be her next series of books she could start reading at home. She laughed at the thought as she walked into the lounge of the Hilton, where the party was being held. She saw Sterling's car there and her stomach dropped. *Why would Sterling and Elizabeth be here?* She walked into the room where the event was being held and saw the two of them immediately. She wanted to turn and run but decided to be big about it all and walked up to them. They both kind of stared at her in disbelief.

"Alex? What on earth are you doing here?" Sterling asked her, shaking her hand.

"Well, I wanted to meet Mr. Williams. He submitted to our company some time ago and I would like him to come work for us. I see he is with Discovery right now."

"Yes, he is. So, you say you have never met him?" Sterling and Elizabeth looked at each other and laughed. Alex looked back and forth at them, puzzled.

"What is the joke?" Ales asked, getting a bit irritated.

"Oh, nothing, Alex, really. Elizabeth, why don't you tell her, it is time for my speech." He kissed Elizabeth on the lips and ran up to the front of the room. Alex looked even more confused.

"Does Sterling know Thomas Williams? What is he speaking about?"

"Alex, did you read the summary of the book at all?" Elizabeth asked.

"Well, of course I did. It is supposed to be this erotic thriller about this complete icy bitch of a woman who ends up getting killed later on in the story or something doesn't she?"

"Ha ha, I can't tell you what happens but I can tell you that this story was written about you, Alex." Alex shot Elizabeth a glare.

"What did you say? How can you possibly know something like that?"
Alex was almost shouting now.

"Because *that* is Thomas Williams." Elizabeth said, pointing and then joining in the applause as Sterling Morris took the stage to announce the release of his new book, one he wrote with one special person in mind. Alex stood there, all color drained from her face as people were hooting and hollering. A few people even came up to her and slapped her on the shoulder, commending her for being such a good sport about it. They all knew. Everyone knew the damn book was about her.

Alexandra Tate had got what she wanted
and now it was being given right back to her.

www.ingramcontent.com/pod-product-compliance
Lightning Source LLC
Chambersburg PA
CBHW051926240626
47153CB00004B/1386